Table of Contents

BE CAREFUL WHAT YOU WISH FOR
WISH FOR
BOOK 1

PETE ANDREWS

ABOUT THE AUTHOR

I write sexy romances. I used to publish under *xleglover* and *Flash of Stocking*.

My stories are romances, so they explore the feelings, emotions and relationships of the characters. My stories are also erotica, so the sex scenes are explicit. Often very explicit.

My stories have an emotional edge to them. The characters have thrilling adventures, but there's pain there too, at least for some of them.

I try to write stories that seem like real life. Yes, the situations are extreme, but I hope you come away thinking, *"Yes, I can see how that might happened."*

Most, if not all, of my stories are based on my real-world wife, Jennifer. She is my inspiration. My muse.

You can find my books wherever e-books are sold. If you'd like to join my mailing list or would like to send me a question or feedback, please email me at *peteandrews1701@gmail.com.*

CAST OF CHARACTERS

Hudson – He's 26. He's gorgeous and has a hot bod. He's a *Master of the Universe* on Wall Street, a sure thing for a lucrative partnership in his company. His favorite movie is *Wolf of Wall Street*. He's in love with Zoey, who (of course) resembles Margot Robbie from the movie.

Zoey – She's 23. She's beautiful and has a slim, toned dancer's body with long shapely legs and small breasts. She's dating Hudson, and they fit together as they are both *Beautiful People*. She's attracted to Hudson because he's a *Real Man* – confident, dominate and controlling. She's a bottom and Hudson is her top.

Greg – He's 26. He works in the same company as Hudson. He's shy, meek and awkward, and has little chance to make partner. Girls might say he's cute, but typically they don't notice him. Greg is tall and has big hands and feet, and those things bode well for another part of his body.

Camilla – She's 45 and the most powerful partner in the company where Hudson and Greg work. In the business world, she's relentless and commanding. They call her the *Dragon Queen*. She has two boys in college. She is a very hot MILF.

Maynard – He's 45 and married to Camilla. He's like an older version of Hudson, with one important exception. He's a professor at Fordham University. Camilla and Maynard are in love, but their relationship is complicated. For one, he has a taste for young flesh.

Sidney – She's 23. She and Zoey are best friends from college. They don't see each other much, as their lives have gotten busy. She's the opposite of Zoey. Brunette, busty, hourglass figure. Careerwise, she's very successful. You might say she's a young Camilla, although she'll never marry. She likes playing the field.

Kimmy – She's 19, an innocent, pretty Chinese girl who has a crush on Greg. She's a college student and works part time in the used bookstore below his apartment. She's also a virgin. Kimmy might seem somewhat familiar to fans of *KT Morrison*, one of my favorite authors.

CHAPTER 1

Hudson lit the pipe and passed it to Zoey. Zoey took a long drag, and then fell back into the sofa and closed her eyes, letting the weed wash over her. In between puffs the pretty blonde sipped her wine, and soon she was in a relaxed haze. It didn't take much for her to get high, as she was a petite girl.

Zoey was 23 and Hudson 26. Hudson had dark hair and was a handsome guy. He had a lean body with a hairless chest.

Zoey was a pretty girl. Her blonde hair and blue eyes gave her an innocent, wholesome look. She had a tight body from years of gymnastics and dance classes. She had little breasts and long beautiful legs.

Hudson and Zoey looked good together. They were one of those "beautiful couples." The kind of couple that people looked at and said "yeah, they should be together, they fit." They'd been dating and exclusive for almost two years. Zoey had moved to New York City after graduating from college to follow her dream to make it on Broadway.

They'd met at a bar, Death & Co., in NYC's East Village. Zoey thought Hudson was the most handsome man she'd ever met. Hudson felt the same about her. She invited him up to her apartment that night. They became inseparable after that, and 6 months later, they were living together.

Zoey liked to look up the meaning of the names of people she knew. Hudson meant *"brave ruler."* She thought that fit her boyfriend. He was masculine, strong and confident, characteristics of a brave man. And Hudson was handsome, charismatic, and a leader, the way a ruler should be.

Zoey felt lucky to be Hudson's girlfriend. He was a major catch. All her girlfriends thought so. They were envious that Hudson was hers.

Hudson caressed his girlfriend's knee, running his fingers over her silky nylons. Zoey's shapely legs never failed to arouse him. His fingers traced up her legs until he reached the bottom of her mini-skirt. Aglow from the pot, she didn't seem to notice. Hudson edged her skirt up, exposing more of her long legs.

Hudson looked over at Greg, and grinned. They were friends and co-workers. Technically they were peers, but Hudson had leapfrogged Greg career-wise. They were nearing a crossroad at their company, as they were both up for partners and there were limited positions available.

Hudson was a slam dunk for partnership, but for Greg things were uncertain. Also, at their company, it was up or out. So, it was very possible that a few months from now, Hudson would be a partner and Greg would be looking for a new job.

But they didn't talk about it, especially not now. Greg's eyes were on Zoey's exposed legs. Hudson loved showing off his girlfriend, and the wine and weed were heightening his passions. He edged Zoey's skirt higher. Zoey realized what was happening and covered Hudson's hands with hers. She tried to push her skirt down, but Hudson playfully tossed her hands aside. Then he kissed her, pulling her towards him. Zoey tried to pull away, but Hudson put an arm around her and covered her mouth with his.

The tussling caused Zoey's skirt to inch up higher. Greg's eyes bulged when he saw the lace of Zoey's stocking tops. He had seen pictures of girls wearing garter belts and stockings on the Internet but had never seen a girl wearing them in real-life.

Zoey wore stockings and garter belts all the time. They made her feel sexy. And Hudson was a major leg man, and she liked dressing up for her man.

Hudson pushed Zoey against the seat of the sofa. As he continued to kiss her, he reached between them and cupped her breasts. Zoey glanced nervously over at Greg and tried to push Hudson's hand away. "No, Hudson" she protested.

"Zoe baby," Hudson cooed as he kissed up her neck. "I can't resist baby. I love you so much. And you're so hot." He pulled her arms above her head and held them there with one hand. With his other he began unbuttoning her blouse. Zoey struggled, trying to wiggle free. "No, Hudson, not here," she whined, her words slurring together because of the weed and wine.

Hudson covered her mouth with his, cutting off further protests. He worked on the buttons until her blouse was completely unbuttoned. He then opened her blouse, exposing her lacy bra and flat tummy.

Hudson grinned at Greg, who was breathing hard and had a huge tent in his pants. Hudson pressed his cheek against Zoey's, turning her head to look at Greg. "I think you've given Greg a woodie," Hudson joke with a chuckle.

"Hudson, stop!" Zoey whined, trying again to break away from his grasp. But Hudson was too strong, and the wine and weed were sapping her strength. Hudson continued to hold her hands above her head. With his other hand he traced the edge of her bra, his fingertips straddling her bare skin and bra. Then he began tracing the lacy patterns in the bra cups. He found her nipple and drew circles around it.

"Nooooo," Zoey whined, trying to wiggle from his touch. Despite herself, she was becoming aroused.

Hudson grinned as Zoey's nipples got hard and poked through her bra. He lowered his head and sucked her nipples through the soft material, causing his girlfriend to moan.

Hudson was incredibly aroused. He liked showing Zoey off – she was so fucking hot – and he often fantasized about another man touching his girlfriend. With his lust fueled by the weed and wine, he found himself motioning to Greg. "Come over here buddy."

Greg walked over – a hard-on apparent in his pants – and sat next to Zoey.

Hudson grinned at Greg. "Doesn't she have great tits? Don't you want to touch them?"

Hudson knew that Greg thought Zoey was hot. He had never come out and said that. Greg was too timid and shy for that. But he knew from the way Greg checked her out whenever he thought no one was looking.

And Hudson also knew that Zoey was fond of Greg. Greg was shy and geeky, and she liked that.

Zoey had a thing about looking up people's names. "Gregory" meant "*shepherd*." Shepherd was a good description of Greg. A nice guy, a hard worker, but shy and passive. He might be a leader of sheep, but not men. Unlike Hudson, who everyone looked up to and followed. Hudson was always the alpha among any group of men.

Hudson's other co-workers were like him, aggressive "Master of the Universe" types. The place they worked – a trading firm on Wall Street – catered to those kinds of personalities. While Zoey wasn't crazy about Hudson's other co-workers, she liked Greg. She wasn't attracted to him physically, but she liked him as a person.

Greg's eyes were locked on Zoey's breasts. His body was frozen though, as he was too timid to take Hudson's invitation to touch her.

When Greg didn't move, Hudson reached over and took his hand. He guided him to Zoey's bra-covered tits. Zoey shook her head as Greg cupped her. She didn't say anything though. Her cheeks were flushed, and she was breathing hard.

Hudson held his hand over Greg's as he showed him how Zoey liked to be touched. "That's it," he said encouragingly. "Like that. Cup and caress her. Rub her nipples between your fingers. They're really sensitive."

Zoey's hard nipples were denting her bra. Hudson watched as Greg rubbed his girlfriend's hard nipple between his thumb and finger through the lace of the bra. "Ahhhh," Zoey moaned, her head rolling back.

Hudson moaned too, as he saw his girlfriend reacting to another man's hand on her. "Yeah, like that Greg," he said to his friend, his voice a lustful, husky whisper. "Keep rubbing her nipples."

"Ahh, ahh," Zoey moaned as Greg did exactly that.

Hudson leaned down and kissed Zoey's lips. Then he moved his mouth to her ear and whispered, "I love you." As he said this, he reached under her and unsnapped her bra. "I love you so much" he said again as he moved his hand to her front and pushed her now loosened bra up off her breasts.

Greg's eyes went wide, and he sucked in his breath as he saw Zoey's naked breasts for the first time. They were perfect. Small yet perfectly formed, like little ripe melons, with perky upturned nipples.

Exposing his girlfriend's breasts to another man's eager eyes inflamed Hudson even more. "Touch her," he said, his voice hoarse and urgent. Then, when it looked like she was about to object, Hudson whispered into her ear, "Zoe baby, it's okay, I'm right here, let him touch you."

Greg's hands were shaking as he tentatively reached out towards Zoey's naked breasts. He felt dizzy as he cupped both her breasts in his hands. Her hard nipples felt like little pencil erasers as they pushed into his palms.

"Suck her nipples, go ahead, suck them," Hudson urged Greg.

Greg looked from Hudson to Zoey. She looked back at him, her cheeks flushed, her lips parted. She looked distressed, but didn't say no. He gently squeezed her breasts. Then he rolled his thumbs over her nipples. Zoey clenched her teeth at his touch and arched her back. Hudson moaned at his girlfriend's reaction to the touch of another man.

"Suck her nipples!" Hudson demanded, his alpha personality coming to the forefront as the lust grew inside him.

Greg felt more confident since Zoey seemed to like what he was doing. He lowered his head and took one of her nipples into his mouth. He cupped and kneaded her breast as he nibbled and rolled his tongue around and over her nipple. It tasted so good! He rubbed her other nipple with his thumb and forefinger.

"Aah aah aah," Zoey moaned as pleasure coursed through her body. Her nipples had always been incredibly sensitive, one of her main erogenous zones. It was like an electric wire from them to her little clit. Hudson had let her hands go, so her fingers clawed at the cushions of the sofa as Greg played with her nipples.

Hudson pressed his lips over Zoey's, and they both eagerly tongued each other. Then she felt her boyfriend slide his hands down her body, over her unbuttoned blouse, and then onto her short, knit skirt. He reached the end of the skirt, his fingertips on her stockinged thighs. Then he curled his fingers around the hem of the skirt. He pulled it up.

"No Hudson ...," Zoey whined, but her protests were lost in Hudson's mouth as he continued to kiss her. She tried to push her skirt back down, but Hudson pushed her hands away. Then, she didn't have the will to protest any more as Hudson pulled her skirt up. Within moments, her legs and panties were completely exposed to Greg's eyes.

"Oh god ...," Greg moaned as he looked at Zoey's exposed legs and panties. She was wearing black stockings with tops of elaborate lace. The tops were stretched where they attached to the straps of her garter belt, which was also black with gold embroidery and edged with delicate lace. Her panties (and her unsnapped bra) matched the garter belt.

All the lingerie was from *La Perla*, the high-end boutique on Madison Avenue across from Central Park. Zoey could never afford such expensive lingerie on her own – she'd had minor roles in a few musicals, mostly part of the chorus. At the moment, she was an unemployed actress. Like thousands of others in New York City, she was looking for her next gig. She was hoping to be "discovered." She didn't have to worry about money though because Hudson was doing well at his job. He loved her, they were a couple and lived together, so he was supporting both of them. As part of that, he was more than happy to buy sexy dresses, high heels and lingerie for his beautiful girlfriend.

Hudson pushed Greg away from Zoey's breasts. Greg was momentarily startled, thinking that his friend had changed his mind and was now pissed.

Hudson replaced Greg's lips on Zoey's nipples, and he pushed Greg to the floor. "Get between her legs," he said between licks of her hard nipples. He gripped her inner thigh and pulled her legs open.

Zoey felt Greg moving between her open legs. "Wait, stop," she gasped, and suddenly it seemed that time stopped. She looked first at Hudson, who was looking back at her. His hand still cupped one of her bare breasts. They were both breathing hard, and Zoey's eyes were heavy-lidded as Hudson rubbed her nipple with his thumb.

Then Zoey looked at Greg. He was on his knees between her parted legs. His eyes were on her legs, and her panties.

With awe in his voice, Greg gushed "You're so beautiful Zoey." The sincerity in his voice charmed her, so she didn't stop him when he put his hands on her thighs. He gently caressed the lace of her stocking tops, and traced his fingertips along the straps of her garter belt, and said (with the same awe in his voice) "This feels so amazing."

Then he placed his palms on the bare skin above her stockings. "Your skin is so soft," Greg said. He looked at Zoey. He looked into her eyes as he said again "You're so beautiful Zoey."

The genuineness and sincerity in Greg's voice disarmed Zoey, and whatever protests she still had ebbed away. Hudson sensed the change in her. He moved his hand to Zoey's panties. She sensed what he was about to do and put her hand over his to stop him. But it was a half-hearted protest, and there was nothing she could do when Hudson curled a finger under her panties and pulled it to the side.

Suddenly Zoey's pussy was exposed to Greg's eyes. Her pussy was a short slit with slim lips on either side, pressed together and a shade darker than the surrounding skin. She kept herself neatly trimmed.

Hudson excitedly looked at Greg looking at his girlfriend's pussy. "Pretty, right?" he said, his voice low and hoarse from excitement.

"Yeah ....," Greg said, his eyes locked on the most intimate part of Zoey's body. Then he looked up at Zoey's face and said, "You're so beautiful." Hudson saw them lock eyes – he saw them share an intimate moment—and for the first time, a twinge of jealousy ran down his spine.

To his surprise, the feeling thrilled him. He didn't understand why. But he was too much in lust to think about it. "Lick her," he told Greg. His voice was a hoarse whisper, but the sexual tension in the room was so high, it was like a shout in a quiet church.

"Hudson ....," Zoey said, shaking her head but not pulling away.

Greg looked unsure. He moved his hands up Zoey's legs, and she sucked in her breath when his fingertips moved from her stockings to the bare skin above. As before, he traced up the straps of her garter belt, stopping just shy of her pussy.

Greg hesitated and looked at Hudson for permission. Hudson nodded his head. Then, with his friend's permission, he lightly rubbed his thumb up and down Zoey's slit.

Zoey was breathing hard, her heart pounding. Her eyes were on Greg as he touched her. He moved his thumb up her slit again, and then stopped there. Greg couldn't see it, but under the hood he felt her clit. It was hard like a pearl. Greg rubbed circles over it.

"Oh god, Greg ...," Zoey moaned as his touch sent waves of pleasure through her body. "Greg ...."

Hudson felt jealous again as he heard his girlfriend say another man's name in the throes of sexual pleasure. Again, the jealousy inflamed him, it made his head spin, it made it hard to breathe. "Lick her," he said again, this time his voice even more urgent.

Greg hesitantly lowered his head and extended his tongue. Hudson felt his girlfriend shudder as his friend began to lick her. "Oh ah ah ah," Zoey moaned as he licked up and down her slit.

"That's right," Hudson said, his voice a husky, urgent whisper. "Lick over her pussy lips. Yes, that's right, like that. Now twirl your tongue around her clit. Yes, like that. Now pull up the skin. See her clit? Lick it. Yeah, like that. Do it again."

"Oh god," Zoey groaned, as Greg licked directly around and over her clit. She squirmed, no longer trying to get away, but in response to Greg's ministrations.

"Now stick your finger into her," Hudson said. "That's right, in and out, finger fuck her. Yeah, like that. She's tight, right? Keep licking her. Now rub your thumb over her clit."

"God, god, oh god," Zoey groaned, her moans coming continuously. She moved her hands down to Greg's head, gripping his hair. "Oh god ......"

"Harder Greg! Lick her clit harder!" Hudson urged. Zoey felt herself going over the edge. She clamped her hands around Greg's head and smashed her pussy into his face. "God, oh god, I'm cumming!"

Hudson's heart pounded in his chest. He couldn't believe he had just seen another guy fondle and eat out his girlfriend. He got on the floor and pushed Greg away. "Move over," he said to Greg as he unbuckled his pants and took out his hard cock. Hudson ripped off Zoey's flimsy panties and then thrust his hard cock inside her. He felt raw and dark, his passions out of control. He smashed his lips against Zoey's, thrusting his tongue into her, just like he was thrusting his cock into her pussy. After just a few moments Hudson came inside his girlfriend.

Hudson collapsed onto Zoey, holding his weight on his elbows. Zoey wrapped her arms around her boyfriend. They were both panting, both thinking about what they'd just done.

But Hudson wasn't done yet. To his surprise, he was still lustful after cumming. He pulled out of Zoey. His cock was already hardening again.

"Take it out Greg," Hudson told his friend. "Let Zoey see it."

Greg was so turned on his body was shaking. Hudson screwing Zoey before his very eyes was the most exciting thing he had ever seen in his life. He got onto the sofa, on his knees, facing Zoey. Then he pulled down his pants. His cock popped out. It was inches from Zoey's face.

Hudson was surprised at Greg's size. While taller, Greg was slim like Hudson. He had assumed a slim guy like Greg would have about the same size penis, especially given how shy and geeky he was.

But Greg's cock was bigger than Hudson's. Noticeably bigger. A couple inches longer, maybe three inches, and thicker. As Zoey stared at Greg's bigger manhood, Hudson felt that tinge of jealousy again.

"Zoe baby," Hudson said, his voice an excited, husky whisper. "Open your mouth."

Zoey looked at her boyfriend. Hudson gave her an encouraging nod. Then she looked back at Greg's cock. She was still breathing hard, her heart was pounding. All this was crazy. Crazy! In the back of her mind, she knew they'd all regret this night, there were always consequences. But now she was just as turned on as Hudson and Greg. And she was curious about this big thing that was inches from her face.

Zoey opened her lips.

All hesitation was gone with Greg. He moved forward, pushing his cock into Zoey's mouth. "Oh god," he groaned as Zoey's soft lips and tongue closed around his cock.

Hudson moaned too, at the sight of another man's cock in his girlfriend's mouth. His cock was hard again, and he began stroking himself. Then Zoey began bobbing back and forth on Greg's shaft, and Hudson's head and cock practically exploded.

This went on for a few minutes, and Hudson sensed that Greg was close to cumming. "Greg, switch places with me," he said. His voice was so hoarse from excitement he was almost hard to understand.

Once again, Greg didn't hesitate. He quickly got off the sofa and moved between Zoey's parted legs. At the same time, Hudson got onto the sofa. He got on his knees just as Greg had been moments before. He pressed his cockhead against Zoey's lips. Normally she'd hesitate to swallow him, as he'd been inside her moments before. But they were past that now. Now she was just as lustful as the men, so she immediately opened her lips and took her boyfriend's cock into her mouth.

Greg was holding his hard cock, the head almost touching Zoey's pussy. He looked at Hudson and the men locked eyes. Hudson nodded, wordlessly giving Greg permission to fuck his girlfriend.

Greg turned back to Zoey and guided his hard cock to Zoey's pussy. When his cockhead touched her pussy, she took Hudson's cock out of her mouth and said, "Greg, you have to use a condom. I'm not on the pill."

Greg didn't seem to understand. He looked questioning at Hudson. Hudson said, "She's allergic to it."

Hudson reached over to the side table, where they kept a box of condoms. He handed one to Greg. He struggled to get it on, because it was a smaller size than he usually used, but eventually he got it rolled down his shaft.

Both Hudson and Zoey were looking at Greg as he sheathed himself. Hudson nodded again at Greg, once again giving him permission. Holding his cock as a guide, Greg positioned his cock between Zoey's pussy lips. Then he pushed in.

Zoey's body tensed as she felt Greg penetrate her. Hudson moaned as he saw another man's cock entering his girlfriend's body.

"Ah ah ah," Zoey moaned as Greg pushed into her. Then she grimaced as it got to be too much, too fast, as he was bigger than she was used to. She put her hand on his chest and said, "Slow, go slow."

Greg went slower, holding himself on his arms as he slowly pushed into her. Eventually he made it all the way in. It was an exertion though and sweat beaded both Zoey and Greg's brows.

Then Greg began moving back and forth, slowly at first, and then faster.

Once again, Hudson felt like he was going to explode. He felt lightheaded. His girlfriend was getting fucked by another man!

"Hudson baby," Zoey said, looking over at Hudson as Greg fucked her. She reached for her boyfriend.

Hudson took her hand. "I love you baby," he said as he squeezed her hand.

"I love you too baby," Zoey said, squeezing his hand back. Then she looked back at Greg. She was breathing hard, panting, her heart pounding. She looked at Greg, into his eyes, as he fucked her.

Hudson let Zoey's hand go and reached over to her breast, cupping her, thumbing her nipple. With his other hand, he rapidly stroked himself. He had never seen anything so hot, and his heart pounded with lustful excitement. "Fuck her, fuck her," he chanted under his breath.

"You feel so good," Greg said as he moved in and out of Zoey's pussy.

"You feel good too," Zoey said, her eyes still locked with Greg's.

Hearing them, seeing them, Hudson again felt jealousy grip his heart. But it was so hot! He stroked himself faster, furiously. Seeing his girlfriend – the girl he loved – fucking another guy was the hottest thing he'd ever seen in his life!

Greg couldn't last much longer. "I'm gonna cum!" he cried. Zoey instinctively wrapped her arms around Greg's neck and pulled him down to her. They kissed as Greg came inside the condom. Hudson moaned at the sight.

Afterwards it was awkward. Greg pulled out and felt embarrassed as he disposed of the condom in some tissues. He hurriedly dressed.

Zoey tugged her skirt down and pulled her open blouse closed, protectively covering her bosom with her arms across her chest. She wasn't able to look at either Hudson or Greg in the eyes.

Hudson wrapped his arms around his girlfriend. He kissed her cheeks and lips, repeating over and over "I love you, I love you, I love you ...."

CHAPTER 2

The next morning, Zoey broke up with Hudson.

She wasn't a prude. She hadn't been a virgin when she met Hudson. She'd lost her virginity in high school. She wasn't a slut (she didn't think so at least), but she'd had a few sex partners before meeting Hudson.

Zoey didn't play hard to get. She didn't play games like that. If she liked a boy, it wasn't hard for him to get into her pants. She was never the aggressor, that wasn't her personality. But if she liked a boy, she was pretty much a sure thing, as long as he had some moves at all. As just one example, she went to bed with Hudson and he was between her legs within just a few hours of meeting him at Death & Co.

Zoey was open to things. She didn't shy away from blowjobs. She liked them actually; she got off on the submissiveness of being on her knees before her man. She didn't spit, she swallowed, except for that one time in her life when it was a one-time hookup with a boy she didn't really like.

She'd done anal. She wasn't crazy about it, but if her man wanted it, she gave it to him. That's how Zoey was. She was all about her man. If she liked a boy, she wanted to keep him happy. Since she didn't just like Hudson but *loved* him – and he was really the first true love of her life – she pretty much did whatever he wanted.

Zoey was a follower, and she'd always been attracted to "take charge" kind of men. That was Hudson. He was very much take charge, very assertive, very much alpha. One of his favorite books was *"Bonfire of the Vanities,"* and he talked about people on Wallstreet being "Masters of the Universe." That was Hudson – he was a Master of the Universe. To Zoey, in fact, Hudson was *the* Master of the Universe.

Also, as Zoey had told all her friends soon after meeting him, "Hudson's freaking gorgeous, he's got a hot bod, and he's super smart and successful." Zoey's friends had been skeptical at first, but after meeting him, they all agreed that Hudson was a major catch. In fact, Zoey had dumped some of her friends when she thought they were trying to steal Hudson from her.

But like everyone, Zoey had limits. She had never cheated on Hudson, she had never cheated on anyone, and if he ever cheated on her, it would kill her.

Before last night, she had never considered having sex with more than one man. She had never considered having a threesome. That's not what good girls did, and Zoey thought of herself as a good girl (at least, that's what she wanted to be).

So, the next morning, Zoey woke up crying. She felt like her life was over. How could Hudson, the man she loved, share her with another man? Didn't he love her? Wasn't he possessive of her? Didn't he want her to be exclusive to him? Was this his way of saying he wanted to be with other girls?

Crying uncontrollably, Zoey threw clothes into a bag and ran from the apartment, even as Hudson tried to reassure her and tell her everything was okay. She went to stay with a friend, another dancer trying to break into Broadway.

Their breakup only lasted a week, with Hudson calling and texting her constantly. They loved each other too much. Zoey loved Hudson too much. She couldn't bear to be without him.

After getting back together, they talked a lot about the night with Greg. They called it "*that night.*"

Zoey had a million questions. She needed to understand what brought it on. Hudson's assurances that he *was* possessive of her even though he shared her with Greg, that he *did* love her even though he got off seeing her with another man, that he had *no* interest in other girls, all those assurances weren't enough for Zoey.

Hudson's words weren't enough for Zoey. She needed to *understand* what made him tick, what was going on inside his head—only if she *understood* would she get the assurance that she needed.

Hudson explained by connecting the dots for her. He said it was all in plain sight if you knew what to look for.

Zoey knew Hudson liked to show her off. She knew he liked her to dress sexy in short skirts and high heels. She knew he liked it when she flashed a little stocking top, or leaned over so men could look down her blouse. She knew he liked it when she flirted. She knew he liked watching her dance with other men. She knew he liked hearing about guys hitting on her. She knew he liked hearing about her old boyfriends, and the kind of sex she had with them.

Zoey had assumed that Hudson was proud to have a pretty girlfriend. She knew she was pretty. It wasn't an arrogant thing. People had told her all her life that she was pretty. And she knew men had big egos, and it was a big ego boost to have a pretty girl in high heels holding onto your arm.

Also, Zoey assumed Hudson liked her to flash and flirt with other men as kind of a way to say *"you can look but you can't touch, she belongs to me."* It was like one-upping other men. Hudson was so dominant about everything, he was so competitive when it came to sports and work, she just assumed this was part of his alpha personality.

And she didn't mind. She liked to flirt, she liked male attention. It was all harmless, and a lot better than an old boyfriend who got insanely jealous whenever another man even looked at her.

Hudson said he didn't understand it himself. Maybe it was because he was a top and Zoey was a bottom. They'd been together for almost 2 years, so they knew that about themselves. Sexually, Hudson got off on controlling Zoey, and she wanted to be controlled. It wasn't bondage with them, they weren't into whips and chains. For them, it was about control.

Like, sometimes Zoey went braless because Hudson told her to. One time at *Jean-Georges,* he made her take off her panties between the appetizer and entrée courses (thank god for long white tablecloths!). Maybe *"that night"* was about that. Hudson got off on forcing her to have sex with another man.

Or, maybe it was because of his parents. It was always about parents, right? Hudson's mom and dad divorced when he was 15, and since then he'd questioned the permanence of relationships. Was it possible for 2 people to love each other forever? So maybe *"that night"* was about Hudson wanting to see how far Zoey would go. Would she do anything for him? Did she love him enough to do anything for him? Even let another man have sex wtih her, if that's what he wanted? And after having sex with another man, would she still love Hudson? Maybe *"that night"* was a test to see how much Zoey loved Hudson.

Hudson told Zoey that he felt intensely jealousy seeing her with Greg, and that made her feel better. It proved he *was* possessive of her.

In the end, Zoey was assured about her relationship with Hudson. *"That night"* was just a bump in the road, it hadn't changed anything. Zoey had already decided that Hudson was the one. She was just waiting for him to ask her.

They'd been dating for 2 years. Her friends were openly asking her when Hudson planned to pop the question. *"Have you talked about marriage?"* they asked her.

But Zoey wasn't the kind of girl to ask a boy about marriage. Just like she'd never ask a boy out on a date. She was traditional that way. Or maybe it was her view of how romance worked. How *she* wanted to be romanced. It was up to the boy to ask.

She was getting worried though. They were still young, she was only 23 (and Hudson 26), but still, 2 years was a long time. Especially since they'd been living together for much of that time.

Zoey worried Hudson would get tired of her. He was around pretty girls all the time. And on Wallstreet, all the girls wore tight skirts, hose and high heels, which she knew better than anyone that he had an eye for. And more than once – way more than once – she'd seen him checking girls out. She told herself that was just a guy thing. All men checked out pretty girls. It was harmless.

But she would worry about it until he put a ring on her finger.

⸺⬥⸺

AFTER THINGS WERE BACK to normal, Hudson risked talking about "*that night*" from a sexual point of view.

"So, how was it?" he hesitantly asked one evening when they were in bed.

"How was what?"

"You know …" Hudson said. "How was it with Greg?"

"You really want to talk about it?" Zoey asked.

"I do."

Zoey looked at her boyfriend. She wasn't surprised, really. Over the last 2 years, he'd asked a lot about her old boyfriends. "It was okay," she said with a shrug.

"You said he felt good," Hudson reminded her.

"Hudson … I don't know what you want me to say," Zoey said with exasperation. "Are you holding this against me now?"

"No, I'm not, I swear," Hudson said, hugging and kissing her. "I just need to know."

Zoey hesitated, then said, "It was fine. It felt good. That's how sex is." Then she quickly added, "It's a lot better with you."

Hudson smiled at her compliment. Then he asked, "Did you cum?"

"No," Zoey said immediately.

"Is that true? Are you lying?"

"I'm not lying Hudson," Zoey said. "I came when he ate me out, but …."

"I just don't want you to say something because you think it'll hurt my feelings," Hudson said. "Just tell me the truth."

Zoey had never orgasmed from intercourse. Which was strange, since she came easily from oral and hand play. But no man had ever made her cum from intercourse.

When Zoey told Hudson that early on in their relationship, he took it as a challenge of course, and for the last 2 years he'd done everything he could to get her off via intercourse. But nothing he did worked.

Hudson was an experienced lover. He was handsome, had the kind of alpha personality that girls (including Zoey) found attractive, and was considered an excellent catch given the schools he went to (Princeton undergrad, Columbia for his MBA) and his success at work. He wasn't the tallest – he was just a couple inches taller than Zoey – but he had a fit, muscular body. So, he had his pick of girls, and had many to practice on before meeting Zoey. And even though he didn't have the biggest penis (he was about 5 inches hard, and average thickness), he never had a girl complain about his sexual prowess. Zoey repeatedly told him he was the best lover she'd ever had.

He tried every position with Zoey, and every technique. But he was never able to make her cum through intercourse. And Zoey didn't fake it either. To her, honestly was everything. She often told Hudson that honesty was the most important thing in a relationship. He agreed with that, because he knew his parents had not been honest with each other and that had been one of the reasons they divorced.

Zoey was worried about Hudson's ego, so she constantly assured him that it was no big deal. She loved sex with Hudson. *LOVE IT!* He *was* her best lover ever, and intercourse with him felt super awesome even if she didn't cum.

Anyways, she got her share of orgasms. Hudson was super considerate, and he never hesitated to go down on her, which made him the *best* boyfriend ever!

And, like the rest of his lovemaking skills, he had a *very* talented tongue. A *freaking awesome* tongue.

"I am telling you the truth," Zoey insisted. "I didn't cum."

Hudson slowly nodded. He didn't show it, but he was relieved. He'd worried that with his bigger cock, Greg had gotten her to cum through intercourse.

Maybe if Greg was a better lover, he would have. That bothered him, but at the same time, the thought made his cock stir, which he didn't understand. Why would he get aroused by the idea of another man making Zoey cum from intercourse, when he couldn't after 2 years of trying?

"So ...," Hudson continued. "Greg's cock is big."

Zoey shrugged but didn't reply.

"Did you notice?" he asked.

"I mean, yeah, I noticed," Zoey said with a nervous laugh.

"So, how did it feel?"

"I don't know," Zoey said with another shrug. She evasively looked down at her feet, not meeting Hudson's eyes. "Honestly, it was actually too much, if anything."

"Really? Because you told him it felt good," Hudson reminded her.

"I mean, I already told you," Zoey sputtered, looking nervous. "That's how sex is."

Hudson looked at his girlfriend. He knew she was holding back, and that bothered him. But what was she not telling him? Had she enjoyed sex with Greg more than she was admitting? The prospect made him feel jealous, but again the jealousy aroused him.

"You looked incredibly sexy with him," he said, trying to make her feel more comfortable. "Seriously. Seeing him on top of you was the sexiest thing I've ever seen."

"Really? Wow," Zoey said looking surprised. "So, you really liked it? I saw you jerking off really hard."

"Yeah, I was," Hudson said, his voice getting husky with arousal. He got on top of Zoey, pushing up the t-shirt she was wearing. It was Hudson's old frat t-shirt. She wore it every night to bed, or one of his other shirts, because he told her early on when they started dating that he liked seeing her wear his shirts.

"I was so hot. I was out of control," Hudson said, kissing her as he cupped her small perky breasts and rubbed her nipples. He pushed down her panties and pushed her legs open with his knee. Usually, he'd spend more time on foreplay (it was no hardship, as she had a hot tight body) but this time he was too hot for that.

He quickly rolled on a condom. He always used condoms, as Zoey wasn't on the pill because of allergies (he had done her bare on *"that night"* and cum inside her, but luckily, she hadn't gotten pregnant).

He pushed his cock into her. He slow fucked his girlfriend as he continued to kiss her and play with her breasts and nipples. When he sensed that Zoey was really into it, he put her long shapely legs over his shoulders and started to fuck her hard.

Hudson was an experienced lover, so he could last a long time. While Zoey didn't cum from intercourse, he knew she liked getting fucked hard, and he was going to give it to her.

Then unexpectantly, images of Greg fucking Zoey appeared in his head. He tried to force the memories away, but they wouldn't stop. It was like a porno movie of *"that night"* playing in his head.

Suddenly, Hudson felt his orgasm building inside him. He couldn't stop it. *"No!"* he shouted inside his head, but there was nothing he could do. He came and shot his sperm into the condom.

He panted as he pulled out and rolled off Zoey. Fuck! He came after just a few moments, like a pimply teenager. He had never come that fast.

"Sorry," he said, feeling embarrassed, as he tossed the condom into the trash.

"Hudson baby, it's okay," Zoey said quickly. "It's a compliment actually."

Hudson frowned as he noted she wasn't even panting. He was mad and embarrassed at himself. He rolled back to her and put his hand on her pussy. He began rubbing her clit.

"I'm okay baby," she said.

"Just let me!" Hudson growled. He immediately felt bad for yelling at her. It wasn't her fault. In a softer voice, he said "Let me make you cum." He played with her pussy, her clit, the way he knew she liked it.

Zoey rolled halfway so now they were on their sides, looking at each other as Hudson jerked her off with his hand. Her eyelids got heavy-lidded and her lips parted, telling him she was getting close. Hudson grinned and said, "You've got your cum face on."

Zoey smiled back at him. "*Cum face*" was one of their secret inside jokes, the kind all couples have. Zoey had her cum face on when she was really aroused.

Then once again, out of nowhere, images of Greg fucking Zoey appeared in his head. He couldn't stop them no matter how he tried. His cock got hard again, and without thinking, he said "Do you want to do it again? With Greg?"

Zoey frowned and immediately said, "No. You're all I want."

"What if I want you to?" Hudson asked.

"Is that what you want?" she asked back.

Hudson hesitated, then admitted "... I'm not sure."

Zoey's eyes widened in surprise. It was so rare to see Hudson looking unsure. He was the freaking Master of the Universe. Hudson was never unsure, he never had doubts.

Hudson's show of vulnerability charmed Zoey. It made her love him more.

But again with Greg? She wasn't sure about that. She *definitely* was not sure about that.

"What you're doing to me, it feels really good," she said, changing the subject. Zoey never lied, but she was good at changing the subject.

Hudson decided not to talk about *"that night"* anymore. He worked on giving her pleasure. A few minutes later she came, arching her back and whimpering as the orgasm flowed through her body.

Hudson was still hard. He rolled on another condom, then got back on top of Zoey. She was surprised, as her boyfriend rarely got hard again so fast after cumming.

Hudson pushed into her. He promised himself he would not cum fast again. Whenever images of Zoey on her back with Greg on top of her crept into his head, he forced them away. This time he was successful.

Hudson made love to his girlfriend, kissing her as he moved in and out. It was passionate too, and he was gratified to hear her moans and pants.

Hudson pulled Zoey's arms above her head. He pinned her hands there and Zoey whimpered. She loved it when he did this. She was submissive, a bottom, and she loved when Hudson – her man – controlled her, took what he wanted from her, used her body for his pleasure.

Hudson used one hand to hold her hands above her head. He used his other hand to finger her clit. They locked eyes as he fingered and fucked her.

When she was close to cumming – and Hudson could always tell when she was close, when she got her cum face on – he allowed himself to cum too. They came together.

Then after, Zoey curled up into his arms, and they fell asleep holding each other.

LATER THAT WEEK

IT WAS CLEAR GREG FELT awkward around Hudson since *"that night."* He avoided Hudson in the office, even to the point of turning the other way if he saw Hudson in the hallway.

Hudson chuckled at that. Greg was a nice guy, but he was a follower, a beta. Greg wasn't a winner. Hudson liked him. But frankly, he was weak, unable to stand up to other men. That was why he probably wasn't going to make partner.

And it was also why Hudson wasn't concerned about Greg having sex with Zoey. After 2 years together, Hudson knew Zoey's type. She was attracted to confident, assertive, strong men. Men who took charge. Alphas. Men like Hudson.

That wasn't Greg at all. He was a nice guy, Hudson liked him, they were friends. But he wasn't at all threatened by Greg.

Hudson wasn't going to ignore what happened, or pretend it didn't happen, or be passive aggressive about it. Losers were passive aggressive. Real men were upfront about things. And that's how he was going to be with Greg.

At Hudson's urging, they went to lunch. Hudson picked the restaurant. After all, he had the unlimited expense account (Greg didn't, which was another sign he wasn't going to make partner).

They went to *Scarpetta.* Honestly, Hudson wasn't crazy about the restaurant. He thought the foliage coming down from the ceiling was gay. And usually there were a few flamboyant dudes there. But it was one of those *"place to be seen"* power lunch spots. And Hudson liked the Branzino.

On top of that, Scarpetta was in the James Nomad hotel, and Hudson had fond memories of JaNo. The day before meeting Zoey, Hudson had fucked a very hot, married cougar in her room at JaNo. She was on business travel in NYC and looking for some extramarital fun. Hudson was happy to oblige, especially when he saw her long legs and sexy stiletto heels. They were red and looked wet, just like her lipstick.

Hudson never told Zoey about this of course. He wasn't stupid. The last thing she wanted to hear was, the day before Hudson fucked Zoey's brains out in her apartment, he was fucking a hot MILF in JaNo.

Hudson was *mostly* faithful to Zoey. But not completely. He couldn't imagine ever being limited to just one pussy, even one as sweet as Zoey's.

Hudson was a good-looking man, and he knew it. He was in the gym almost every day to keep his body hard and muscular. Also, he was successful and well dressed in mostly expensive Italian suits, although he had a few suits made by bespoke clothiers in London.

So, Hudson had a lot of opportunities for pussy. He liked variety. Zoey was blonde and petite with small breasts. So, when he stepped out, his eyes were on curvy brunettes and redheads with big tits. He never felt guilty about cheating. He was a *Master of the Universe*. He was entitled.

Hudson made sure Zoey never found out, or even suspected. He loved Zoey. He was probably going to marry her.

A few times though, Hudson had taken Zoey to Scarpetta, because Italian was her favorite food. She actually liked the flaming gay foliage falling from the ceiling. Not that he ever made gay jokes in front of her. She was a leftwing democrat. Fox would probably call her a radical liberal. *Whatever.* Hudson didn't care about politics, not with her. With her looks, her tight bod, and her sweet personality, she could be a socialist and he wouldn't care. Anyway, whenever they went to Scarpetta, they always had great sex after and usually Hudson thought about that sexy MILF as he fucked his pretty, leggy girlfriend Zoey.

Hudson got a scotch. Highland Park.

Greg ordered a Cosmo. Really? A pink drink? Hudson laughed inside. But he didn't make fun of the guy. He wasn't a jerk. Well, that wasn't quite true. Hudson *was* a jerk, at least sometimes. But he wasn't an asshole.

"So, Greg," Hudson began once their drinks arrived. "We need to talk about that night."

"Hudson, are you pissed at me?" Greg timidly asked. He was clearly scared.

"I'm not pissed at you Greg," Hudson said. "If I was pissed, I would've punched you in the face. Have I punched you in the face?"

"You sound like you're pissed," Greg said warily.

Hudson laughed. "I'm not pissed," he assured his friend. "But let's make sure we're on the same page. You owe me now. So, when you get a girlfriend, a girl you really like, I get to fuck her. Then we'll be even. Okay?"

Greg's eyes went wide with shock and alarm.

Hudson laughed. "I'm just fucking with you," he said with a grin. "Shit, if I ever fucked another girl, Zoey would seriously cut off my dick. And I'm not even kidding. She gets insane when she's jealous. She's hot though when she gets mad."

It was true. That was another reason he made sure Zoey never found out about his extracurricular activities.

Still grinning, Hudson said "She's hot, right? You think she's hot?"

"Everyone thinks Zoey's hot," Greg said, looking nervously down at his feet.

Suddenly the memory of this man on top of his girlfriend flashed into Hudson's head. Her blouse was open, her bra unsnapped. Her skirt bunched up around her waist. Her panties lay somewhere on the floor. Greg was fucking her, Zoey's long shapely legs wrapped around his waist. She still wore the garter belt, the stockings. Her pretty feet were pointed as he pounded her pussy. Zoey panted into Greg's face as he fucked her.

Hudson's cheeks flushed at the memories. He gulped down the Highland Park and composed himself. He said, "Will you be at happy hour tonight?" The young people from their firm – the 20- and 30-somethings – typically went to happy hour on Friday nights.

"I wasn't planning to," Greg sourly said with a shrug. Hudson understood. It was humiliating for Greg to be around their co-workers since it was common knowledge that he probably wasn't on partnership track.

"You should come," Hudson told him. "Zoey'll be there. You can hang with us."

CHAPTER 3

Zoey hesitated when she saw Greg with Hudson and the rest of their co-workers at the happy hour. But people had already seen her and were calling her over, so she had no choice but to join the group.

It had been a month since *"that night."* She felt awkward seeing Greg, and it was clear he felt awkward too.

Zoey gave hello kisses to people she knew. Then she gave Hudson a hug and a more lingering *"girlfriend"* kiss. Then it was time to say hello to Greg. People knew they were friends, so they would wonder if she didn't say hello. And rumors were the last thing Zoey wanted now.

While still holding Hudson's hand, she halfway turned her body, so she was sorta facing Greg. She forced a smile and said, "Hey Greg."

"Hi," Greg said back. He looked wary, like he didn't know what to do.

Zoey got on her tiptoes to give him a hello peck on the cheek. Even in high heels, she still had to get on her tiptoes because he was much taller.

Hudson found himself breathing harder. He suddenly realized that things were different. All the men in the bar, they were checking his hot girlfriend out, undressing her with their eyes, wondering what it felt like to touch her, to be inside her. But Greg *had* seen Zoey's body. He *had* touched her. He *did* know what it felt like to be inside her pussy.

"Are you okay?" Zoey asked him. She was looking worriedly at his face. "Are you feeling okay?"

Hudson grabbed her arm. "Come on, you need a drink," he said. He led her to the bar.

"She'll have a Belvedere martini, no vermouth, extra dirty, with olives. Softly shaken," Hudson told the bartender. "And I'll have another Highland Park. One ice cube."

Zoey stared at Hudson. It wasn't because he was ordering for her. He *always* ordered for her. She liked that.

It was because she was wondering what he was thinking about. He seemed distracted. And anxious.

That wasn't like her boyfriend. Hudson was never anxious.

The drinks arrived and Zoey took a sip of the dirty martini. She was waiting for her boyfriend to say something.

Hudson looked back at his girlfriend. He abruptly said, "Greg and I talked about it today."

"Is that what we're calling it now? *It?*" Zoey joked with a slight smile.

Hudson smiled back, then said "He said he thinks you're very hot."

Zoey's smile turned into a *"deer in the headlights"* look.

"I told him to come to happy hour tonight," Hudson continued. "I told him he could hang with us. With you and me."

Zoey's eyes went wide, realizing where this was going. She took a big gulp of the martini, finishing it. Hudson ordered her another one.

"I'm going to talk to Greg," Hudson told his girlfriend as her new drink arrived. "Why don't you be my social butterfly while I'm talking to him?" It was another one of their inside jokes – Zoey was outgoing and liked to socialize, she would literally talk with anyone, and Hudson had taken to call her "his social butterfly."

Hudson walked over to Greg. He saw he was checking Zoey out as she talked to some of their co-workers. "She looks good tonight, right?" Hudson asked.

Zoey was wearing a fitted white blouse over a black pencil skirt. The blouse was tight across her breasts and the skirt ended a couple inches above her knees. She wore black hose and black high heels. Because she knew she'd be seeing Hudson's co-workers, she'd curled her long blonde hair and spent extra time on her makeup. She wanted to look extra pretty for her boyfriend. And she did look pretty. So hot and beautiful she looked like a movie star or supermodel.

Greg didn't answer but he was ogling Zoey with his eyes. Hudson saw his eyes drift to her long shapely legs, and he said "Yes, she is."

"What?" Greg asked, not understanding.

"You're wondering if Zoey's wearing stockings and a garter belt, like the other night," Hudson said. "Yes, she is. That's what she usually wears. She says it makes her feel sexy. And she knows I like it."

Greg gulped. "You shouldn't be telling me this," he said.

"Why?"

"Because it's private things she's told you," Greg said. "You're her boyfriend. I shouldn't know these things."

"But you've been intimate with her," Hudson reminded him.

Greg gulped again.

"Can I ask you a personal question?" Hudson said.

When Greg nodded, Hudson asked "When were you with a girl last? I mean, before that night?"

Greg looked embarrassed. "I don't know. A long time," he admitted. Looking sheepish, he said "This partnership thing has kinda killed my confidence. You know?"

Hudson gave him a sympathetic nod. "And since then, have you been with a girl?" he asked.

Greg shook his head no.

"But you're still a man," Hudson said. "You have needs."

"Why are you saying this?" Greg asked with exasperation.

Hudson swallowed hard. His cock was uncomfortably erect in his pants. "I'm just saying, you needed Zoey that night. You needed her body. To take care of your needs."

Greg stared at Hudson.

"Am I right?" Hudson asked. His voice was husky with lust.

Greg hesitated. Then he nodded yes.

"And now you haven't had a girl since then," Hudson said.

Greg didn't reply. Like Hudson, he was breathing hard.

"She likes her neck kissed," Hudson said. "Start at her shoulder, then kiss up her neck, to her ear, to behind her ear. Just below her ear. It drives her crazy."

Greg stared at Hudson.

"You already know her nipples are super sensitive," Hudson continued. "Her knees are really sensitive too. Not the back of her knees though. That's usually too much for her. But when you're inside her, if you put her legs on your shoulders, she likes it then. She likes it if you caress the back of her knees while you're fucking her."

"Why are you telling me this?" Greg hissed in a low voice. His face looked pained, like Hudson was torturing him.

"Do you want to be with her again?" Hudson asked.

Greg's eyes went wide. "Are you serious?" he asked incredulously.

"Do you need my girlfriend's body again?" Hudson asked as he stared in Greg's eyes. "To take care of your needs? If you want to do this, you have to answer me, Greg."

Greg hesitated, like he was wondering if this was some kind of trap. Then he said "Yes."

Hudson nodded. "But you need to understand," he said. "She belongs to me. So, I'm in control. You do as I say. Do you agree?"

Greg nodded as he said, "Yes."

"We shouldn't be seen leaving together," Hudson said, glancing around at their co-workers. He didn't want rumors any more than Zoey. "You leave now. We'll meet you at our apartment."

Greg was about to leave when Hudson grabbed his arm. He said, "Greg. On the way, buy some condoms. In your size. You never fuck Zoey without a condom. She's not on the pill."

Greg stared at Hudson. Both men were breathing hard. Greg nodded. Then he turned towards the exit.

When Greg was gone, Hudson looked across the room at Zoey. She was looking back at him. Clearly, she'd been watching the two men talk.

With a slight movement of his head, he motioned to where Greg had gone. Zoey's expression turned into that *"deer in the headlights"* look again, and she gulped down the rest of her martini.

<hr>

THEY WERE IN AN UBER on the way to their apartment. "Hudson, I don't know about this," Zoey whispered doubtfully.

"Greg is having a hard time meeting girls," Hudson whispered back. "He knows he's not making partner, and that's killed his confidence. You know how he is. He's shy. I can't exactly see him getting on Tinder."

"I feel bad for him," Zoey said honestly. "But how does that affect us?"

Hudson looked into Zoey's eyes as he whispered, "Before that night, he hadn't been with a girl for a long time. He told me. He has needs though. All men do. He needed you to take care of his needs."

Zoey's eyes opened wide. Her lips parted.

Hudson hugged his girlfriend, feeling her tight sexy body under her sexy outfit. He whispered into her ear, "Zoe baby, Greg needed your body to take care of his needs. And now he needs you again. He said so."

"He told you that?" Zoey asked incredulously.

Hudson nodded. "Zoe baby, he needs your body again, to take care of his needs. And I'm giving you to him. For tonight. He's my friend. You're going to let Greg use your body to take care of his needs."

Zoey swallowed hard at her boyfriend's words. Then she shook as a shiver ran though her. "You really want this?" she asked.

"Yesssss," Hudson hissed lustfully.

"It really gets you hot?"

"Yesssss," he hissed again.

"But you have to promise," Zoey said desperately. "If I do this again, it won't affect us. You'll still love me. It won't affect us. Do you promise?"

"I promise Zoe baby," Hudson said, hugging his girlfriend tight and kissing her. "I'll always love you. I promise."

—◉—

"I WANT YOU TO KISS," Hudson told them.

They were in their apartment. Zoey was sitting on the sofa next to Greg. Hudson was sitting across from them, in an armchair.

Hudson owned the apartment. He bought it with cash from his bonus checks. He had just started dating Zoey, and she was very impressed. *Very* impressed. No one *owned* their apartment in New York City. At least, no one she knew. And it was a big apartment. Two bedrooms, two full baths, modern kitchen, and separate living and dining rooms. The apartment was evidence of how successful Hudson was, and everyone knew his potential on Wall Street was unlimited.

She didn't know anyone who was as successful as Hudson. And he was young, just 3 years older than her. All her friends were aspiring dancers and actors, living in groups of 4 or 5 in small ratty apartments. All except her. She lived with Hudson in his glamorous apartment.

Zoey had no money. She relied on her pretty looks to get into clubs for free and men to buy her drinks. So, when Hudson called his bank to transfer the money to pay for the apartment – the way *freaking* Jeff Bezos would do it! – she was awed.

And Hudson was so handsome. *So* gorgeous! Zoey was certain he was the most handsome man she had ever met.

The day after she slept with Hudson after meeting him at Death & Co, she was afraid he wouldn't call her, that she had been too easy. She squealed – literally squealed! – when he called her later that week and asked her out. She was head over heels almost immediately. When he asked her to move in with him, it was the happiest day of her life.

Zoey waited for Hudson to say the L word first. But really, she fell in love with him at Death & Co, when he looked at her with his beautiful dark eyes.

For her part, Zoey kept Hudson happy. Zoey didn't have that much going for her. Not really. She wasn't book smart. She barely graduated from college. She needed a calculator for any kind of math. Seriously. *Any* kind of math. And to be honest, she wasn't that talented as a dancer.

But she had a pretty face. Maybe even a beautiful face. She had a firm body, a tight ass, and long legs. Her breasts were small, but – and this proved they were meant to be together – Hudson preferred girls with little tits. Hudson called her tits her *"little high school breasts."* It was another one of their inside jokes. And it wasn't an insult. It delighted Hudson that she was often carded in bars and restaurants. He liked to joke she was his barely legal girlfriend.

And Zoey knew how to make a man happy. Like wearing stockings and heels. And when she was on her period, she gave her man plenty of blowjobs. Like, every day. More if he wanted. And she always swallowed. Although, sometimes, Hudson liked to see it dribble out of her mouth and down her chin. Or cum on her face. Hudson was a bad boy. That was something else she loved about him.

Zoey loved his (*their!*) apartment. Hudson owned it, but she thought of it as hers too. The apartment was in a converted warehouse in TriBeCa, so all the apartments in the building had exposed brick walls and high ceilings.

Because the apartments had high ceilings, they were advertised as "loft apartments" even though none of the apartments had lofts. Still, Hudson and Zoey called their home their *"loft apartment."* It was another one of their inside jokes. It was part of the culture of their relationship.

They could walk to so many wonderful restaurants. Tribeca Grill, the famous restaurant owned by Robert De Niro, was one of their favorites. They met him once while dining there. They met Robert De Niro!

They also liked Nobu. Zoey had never had sushi until Hudson took her there. She practically had an orgasm the first time she tried sea urchin. It was so freaking amazing!

She loved their loft apartment! She loved their neighborhood!

And now she was sitting on the sofa with Greg, in their loft apartment. And Hudson wanted her to kiss him. He wanted her to kiss another man.

It was ... so ... fucking ... crazy.

"I want you to kiss," Hudson said again.

Zoey looked hesitantly at Hudson, and then Greg. He looked as hesitant as her. She looked back at Hudson. He gave her an encouraging smile and nod.

Zoey had misgivings about this. But it was what her boyfriend wanted her to do. And it was her goal in life to make Hudson happy.

She looked back at Greg. He still looked hesitant. She gave him an encouraging smile, just as Hudson had given her. Then she leaned in towards Greg. She was happy to see him leaning into her too. This would be easier if she didn't have to lead him. If she didn't have to control him. She didn't know how to do that. She was always the one being controlled. She was submissive. A bottom. It would be weird for her if she had to be a top because Greg was a bottom.

But then she realized that Hudson was controlling both her and Greg. He was the top and they were both bottoms. To him. That made Zoey feel better.

Zoey closed her eyes. She always closed her eyes when she kissed a boy. They leaned closer. And then their lips touched. They nibbled at each other's lips. Then their lips parted slightly, and they pressed harder. Still soft, but harder. They were kissing. Making out.

"Oh god," Hudson moaned as he watched the girl he loved kissing another man. Jealousy spiked inside him. It hurt but, it was delicious too. He held a tumbler in his hand. He took a long gulp of the Highland Park scotch.

Hudson watched as Zoey put her hand up behind Greg's head. She ran her fingers through his hair as they continued to kiss.

"Wow, Jesus, wow," Hudson said under his breath. Then he saw Zoey's cheek move. Greg's tongue was in her mouth. They were tonguing each other. "Oh gaaawd," Hudson groaned, bending forward like in pain.

When he looked up, they were looking at him. They were both panting. Zoey's cheeks were flushed. Her hand was still around Greg's neck. "Are you alright?" she asked with her sweet voice.

"Yesssss," Hudson said, his voice a lustful hiss. "Keep going."

Zoey got up and walked over to Hudson. She sat down next to him. She hugged him. Then, with their faces close together, she whispered "We don't have to do this. We can stop. Greg can go home, and we can go to bed."

Hudson shook his head no. "Go back and sit with Greg," he told her.

Zoey sat back with Greg. "Closer," Hudson said. Zoey slid closer to Greg until their hips almost touched.

"Greg," Hudson said. "Unbutton her blouse."

Greg eagerly reached for Zoey's front. He unbuttoned her blouse to her skirt. Then he boldly pushed the blouse off her shoulders, completely exposing her bra covered breasts. Kissing Zoey had given him more confidence. He was pretty sure she'd been into it, as he'd heard her moan, although her moans had been so soft, he doubted Hudson heard them.

"Zoey, look at me," Hudson ordered. "Pull your hair to the side. Let Greg see your neck. Yeah, like that. Now Greg ... kiss Zoey's neck. Like I told you."

"You told Greg what I like?" Zoey asked incredulously.

Hudson nodded. Looking at his girlfriend, he said "Greg needs your body to take care of his needs. But I want you to enjoy it too."

Zoey's lips parted as she stared at her boyfriend.

"Greg, kiss Zoey's neck," Hudson ordered again. Then he said in a softer voice, "Zoe baby ... keep looking at me."

Zoey had a blank expression on her face as Greg began kissing her. Following Hudson's earlier instructions, he started at her shoulder, at her bra strap. Then he kissed across her shoulder, then moved up her neck.

Greg had soft lips and he nibbled and lightly dabbed with the tip of his tongue as he kissed her. He took his time, and his patience surprised Hudson. His efforts worked, because as he reached halfway up Zoey's neck, her blank expression changed. Her lips parted and she began breathing harder.

Her eyelids got heavy as Greg's lips neared her ear. Hudson called it her *bedroom eyes*, and it was a sure sign of her arousal. Zoey was getting her cum face on.

Zoey kept her eyes on Hudson as her breathing got heavier and her cheeks more flushed. The entire time, he felt a big vise around his heart, as he watched another man kissing and arousing his girlfriend.

Then Greg reached her ear. A little bit below and behind her ear. He lingered there, kissing, nibbling, softly licking. Zoey's eyelids fluttered, as she kept her eyes on Hudson and tried to pretend like everything was normal. But her breathing got harder and her cheeks more flushed. Her face looked strained. Hudson knew what he was seeing. Another man was seducing his girlfriend.

"God, yeah, god, this is good, god, this is good," Hudson moaned under his breath. Seeing another man arousing Zoey in front of his eyes was so exciting. He put his hand on his crotch and rubbed his hard cock through his pants.

"Greg," Hudson began, his voice hoarse through arousal. "Put your hand on Zoey's breast. Cup her. Rub her nipple with your thumb."

Zoey's bra was midnight black. The bra was mostly black lace with metal underwire, and unlined. Early on in their relationship, Hudson had mentioned that he thought blonde girls in black lingerie were hot. Since then, she had mostly worn only black lace under her clothes. For Hudson.

Zoey's perky nipples were upturned. At the moment, they were hard like little pencil erasers. They dented the wispy lace of the bra. Hudson knew it was Greg (not him) who got her nipples hard like that, and that knowledge made him dizzy with jealousy and lust.

He watched as Greg, who was still nibbling at Zoey's neck, reached for her breast. Zoey clenched her jaw when she felt him cup her. Then he rolled her nipple with his thumb, through the lace of her bra, and she finally lost her composure. She rolled her head back and whimpered "oh oh oh oh oh ...."

"Oh jeez, oh jeez, that's good, that's good," Hudson moaned as he watched his girlfriend respond to Greg's lips and fingers. "Greg, Greg," he groaned. "Her bra. Unsnap her bra. Take it off."

Greg first pulled Zoey's blouse off her arms. Then he reached behind her with both hands. Greg fumbled awkwardly with the snap. It took him a few tries to unsnap it. Finally he pulled off the bra and tossed it onto the floor. It landed next to her white blouse.

Hudson moaned at the sight in front of him. The previous time – the first time – Zoey had kept her blouse and bra on, even though they were open and unsnapped. Now though, she was completely naked from the waist up with another man. With another man. And she was responding to him.

"Touch her breasts Greg," Hudson ordered with a lust filled husky voice. "Suck her nipples."

Greg cupped her bare breasts, her little high school breasts. He gently kneaded and caressed them. Then he lowered his head and sucked one of her nipples into his mouth.

"Mmmph ...," Zoey moaned. She tried to keep eye contact with Hudson, but then she lost it. She wrapped her arms around Greg's head and pulled him against her bosom. "Oh god, Greg, oh god ...," she moaned.

The vise squeezed Hudson's heart harder as he heard his girlfriend say another man's name. "Yeah, that's good, so good, yeah," he softly whimpered under his breath. "Say his name, say his name ..."

After a few moments of Greg fondling and kissing Zoey's breasts, Hudson said "Greg, reach behind Zoey and unzip her skirt."

Greg moved his hands around Zoey's waist but she said, "It's on the side." She was breathing hard, panting. She reached to her side and pulled down the zipper. Greg tried to pull the skirt down, but it was too tight to pull down sitting the way they were.

Zoey got off the sofa and stood up. She faced Hudson, looking into his eyes. "That's it Zoe baby," he said, nodding encouraging at her. "You're doing so good. Now take off your skirt. I want Greg to see you."

Hudson pulled his chair closer so he had a better view.

Zoey looked into his eyes as she shimmied the tight pencil skirt down her long legs. Then it was puddled around her high heeled feet. Since she was still facing Hudson, Greg was able to see her backside. She wore a black garter belt, black stockings and black panties. The panties were a thong, and the material was bunched between her cheeks, so it was like her ass was naked, fully exposed to Greg's eager eyes.

"Zoey, god, so hot," Greg said with his eyes locked on her tight ass framed by the garter belt. His face burned with lust. Suddenly, he fell to his knees behind her. He was frenzied, out of control. He grabbed her hips with both hands, pulling her cheeks apart. Then with his thumb, he managed to reach into her exposed crack and pull the thong to the side.

For a moment, Greg looked at what he had exposed. Zoey was completely hairless there. Like the rest of her body, the skin was soft, smooth and unblemished, although light in color since this was a part of her that never saw the sun. His eyes focused on her little puckered asshole. That's when he really lost it. He frantically pressed his nose into her crack and began licking.

"Oh oh oh," Zoey whimpered as she felt Greg's tongue on her most intimate parts. Her knees weakened, so she grabbed Hudson's shoulders for support. With her body shuddering, she whimpered "Greg ... Greg's licking my ass ...."

"Oh god, oh god ..." Hudson gasped. "Greg, you're nasty. So nasty."

Greg moved his hand to her front. He edged his fingers into her panties, and quickly found her clit. "Mmmmph ahhhhh ahhhhh," Zoey moaned, her head rolling back. Greg was rubbing her clit as he licked her ass.

"Oh god, shit, shit, oh god, Greg ...," Zoey moaned. "I'm cumming ... oh shit ... I'm cumming, I'm cumming ...."

Then Zoey collapsed onto Hudson as her body shook, an intense orgasm ripping through her tight sexy body.

Hudson was startled. Things had moved so fast. What Greg had done was unexpected. Licking her ass while rubbing her clit? Hudson had never done that to his girlfriend. He didn't like ass play. Well, he liked *getting* it, but not doing it. And, as far as he knew, no man had ever done Zoey that way. Greg was the first to do that to her, the first to make her cum that way.

For the first time, Hudson wondered if he had underestimated Greg. He wondered if it was a mistake to share his girlfriend with him.

Greg abruptly stood up. He grabbed Zoey by her shoulders and pushed her onto the sofa. She fell onto her back, looking up at Greg, a surprised look on her face.

Greg frantically tore off his clothes. His cock was hard. He threw Zoey's legs apart and then pulled her panties to the side. Her approached her pussy with his cock in his hand.

"Oh god, yeah, that's good, that looks so good," Hudson panted as he saw Greg press the knob of his big cock against Zoey's pussy lips. Then he rubbed his cock up and down her slit, lubricating himself. "Oh wow, wow, Jesus, yeah, that's so good, so good," Hudson panted.

"You're going to use her now, right Greg?" Hudson said lustfully. "You're going to use my girlfriend's body for you needs, right Greg?"

"Yeah, yeah, that's right," Greg answered, his voice husky with lust like Hudson's.

"You hear that baby?" Hudson asked. "You okay with that?"

"Oh yeah, yeah," Zoey said. She was as lustful now as the two men. She was in major sub-space now, and the idea of being used like an object – like a piece of meat – to satisfy a man's needs tickled her submissive desires.

Zoey looked at Greg and said, "Use me, Greg. Use my body. Use Hudson's girlfriend to take care of your needs."

"Oh god Zoe baby!" Hudson moaned at her words. He had his cock out now and was stroking himself. "That's so good! So good!"

Greg pushed into Zoey. They both grunted at the penetration. "God, so tight Zoey," he groaned.

Zoey put a hand on his chest and said, "Slow Greg."

Greg pushed in slow. "Mmmph ah ah mmph ah ..." Zoey groaned as he slowly penetrated her. His cock got thicker at the base, so the deeper he pushed, the more he stretched her open. "Wow, god, wow, wow ...," she gasped as Greg pushed in deeper. He was stretching her pussy more than any man have ever done before. And with his long cock, he was going in deep too.

This was different than the first time with Greg. That time, she had been high and drunk. Now she was mostly sober, even after drinking at the happy hour. Now she really noticed how thick Greg's cock was, and how long.

Greg began slow, short in and out movements, each time pushing in deeper. Zoey panted, looking into Greg's eyes as he penetrated her body more and more. She sucked in her breath and groaned each time he moved in and out.

Then Zoey realized she was paying too much attention to Greg, at the expense of her boyfriend. She looked at Hudson. She saw he had his cock out and was stroking himself. She reached for his hand, saying "Hudson baby, hold my hand ...." Hudson took her hand but continued to jerk off with his other hand.

"You're doing really good baby," Hudson told her. "You look so sexy with Greg's cock in you."

"That's what you want?" she asked. She needed assurance again that this wouldn't affect their relationship.

"Yes!" Hudson lustfully hissed. "This is. So. Fucking. Hot!"

Greg finally got all the way in. As he pushed the last inch into her – the thickest inch – Zoey grimaced and squeezed Hudson's hand hard. "Oh god!" she groaned, a wince in her pretty face.

"Is Greg's big cock too much baby?" Hudson asked her, reminding her what she said about the first time.

"It *is* too much," Zoey said back, perspiration covering her brow from the exertion. Then she looked at Greg and added, "But it's okay, it's—"

At that moment, Greg pulled out halfway, then pushed back in.

"Oh fuck!" Zoey grunted. Greg did it again and she moaned "Ohmygaaaawd!"

Then Greg began fucking her faster, and harder. He leaned forward on his elbows, his chest pressing down on Zoey's breasts. Their faces were barely an inch apart. They panted into each other's mouth.

With Greg positioned that way, his cock was rubbing up Zoey's walls, as opposed to down. She didn't realize it at the time, but his cock was rubbing against her g-spot.

Zoey felt something building inside her. It was an unfamiliar sensation; she had never felt this inside her before. Then with a start, she realized what it was. She was nearing a vaginal orgasm! Greg was going to make her cum from intercourse!

Hudson's eyes were on Greg's cock pistoning in and out of Zoey's pussy. He was fucking her hard, like a battering ram. As he watched, Hudson rapidly jerked his cock. It was like last time, he was in a frenzy, he felt out of control.

Greg was moaning hard. Hudson sensed he was close to cumming. Then he realized something, and his head practically exploded.

"Greg you mother fucker!" Hudson yelled. "You're not wearing a condom!"

"What? What?" Greg said. He didn't stop fucking Zoey. "I'm sorry ...."

"Pull out you fucker!" Hudson yelled. "Don't you dare cum inside her!"

Greg forced himself to pull out. "I'm sorry, I forgot, I'm sorry ...," he said.

"You fucking forgot?!" Hudson yelled incredulously. "You mother fucker!"

As Hudson glared and yelled at Greg, he didn't notice the look on Zoey's face. She looked bewildered and confused. She also looked disappointed. She'd been about to cum. She'd been on the brink. Greg pulled out just as she was about to cum. It would've been the first time. The first vaginal orgasm of her life.

"Hudson, Hudson, I'm sorry, I really forgot," Greg pleaded. He reached for his pants and pulled out a condom. "I bought condoms, just like you said. See? I just forgot. I'm sorry, man."

Greg's words seemed to placate Hudson somewhat. At least he stopped yelling.

Zoey looked at the condom in Greg's hand. The label said "Magnum XL." Hudson's condoms said "Regular Size."

"Would it be okay, I mean, can I finish?" Greg meekly said to Hudson. "I was just about to cum." He quickly ripped open the condom package and rolled the condom onto his shaft. "Can I?"

Before Hudson could answer, Zoey reached for Greg's cock with her hands. "I can finish him this way, okay?" she asked. She was looking at Hudson. She was asking her boyfriend, not Greg.

Hudson considered a moment. Then he nodded his head yes.

Zoey rolled the condom off and began stroking him with both hands. Greg groaned at the touch of her soft hands.

Zoey had not wanted to let Greg back inside her. She was still coming to grips with what almost happened. If Greg made her cum through intercourse, she'd feel like she was betraying Hudson. It would be like cheating on him. Hudson should be the first man to make her cum that way. Or if not him, then no one should.

As Zoey stroked Greg, she looked at Hudson and mouthed "I love you."

Hudson mouthed back "I love you too."

Then Greg came, splattering Zoey's stomach with his cum.

CHAPTER 4

The next week, Greg approached Hudson. He went into Hudson's office and closed the door.

"Hudson, I wanted to apologize again about the other night," he said. "About not using a condom."

Hudson frowned at Greg, but he was no longer angry. After all, things turned out all right since he pulled out. "I don't want to have to remind you each time," he said sternly.

Greg brightened. "You mean we'll do it again?" he asked hopefully.

"I don't know," Hudson said. "I'm just saying, if it does, I don't want to have to remind you. You just do it. I've told you. Zoey's not on the pill. She's allergic to it."

"So ... is Zoey mad at me?" Greg asked hesitantly. "I thought she got off on it."

Hudson's eyes narrowed. "Be careful what you say Greg," he said harshly. "This is my girlfriend you're talking about. Don't get any ideas."

"I'm sorry, I'm sorry," Greg said, his hands out in surrender.

Hudson shook his head. He couldn't believe how easy Greg gave into things. How quickly he surrendered. Not just this but everything. It was like the dude didn't have a backbone. How did he ever wind up on Wall Street?

"Look," Hudson said with a conciliatory tone. "We're dudes, we can enjoy things for what they are, we don't over analyze things. But Zoey, well, she's a good girl. So, she's trying to get her head around it. That's what's going on. Zoey's trying to get her head around it. I'm not saying it's gonna happen again, or not gonna happen. We'll just have to see." Then Hudson trained a hard glare at Greg and said, "If I hear you bragging about this, I will seriously kick your ass."

"Hudson, Hudson, come on, I would never do that, I won't say anything," Greg said, his hands out in surrender again. "Can I ... can I tell you something?"

Hudson clenched his jaw, feeling impatient. Greg was a nice guy, but sometimes he was *too* nice. Why ask permission to say something? Get a fucking backbone and just say it!

"Sure, go ahead," Hudson said, doing his best to hide his irritation.

"After being with Zoey, well ...," Greg sputtered, both nervous and embarrassed. "What I'm trying to say is, once you get *some* sex, you want it more, you know? So, I've been going out to try and meet a girl ...." His voice trailed off dejectedly.

"No luck buddy?" Hudson asked, giving his friend a sympathetic smile.

Greg shook his head. He shrugged and said sheepishly, "The bar scene's not really my thing."

"Have you tried Tinder?"

Greg looked down at his feet. "I can't see myself doing that," he said.

Then, still looking at his feet, he sputtered, "So, I mean ... I still have needs ... and if you and Zoey are up for it ... I mean, if Zoey is, and if you don't mind ... you know what I'm saying Hudson?"

"You want to use her again," Hudson said, staring at Greg, his throat suddenly dry from arousal. "You want to use my girlfriend's body again, to take care of your needs."

Greg still wasn't able to look Hudson in the eyes, but he nodded.

———●———

A MONTH WENT BY AND Zoey didn't want to do it again. They talked about it though. Hudson liked to talk about it, he got off on it, and this (talking about it) was something Zoey could do for her man.

"I guess I don't get it," Hudson said one evening when they were in bed. They were on their sides, looking at each other. "What we're doing is fun. We're young. We're sowing some wild oats. How is this not a good thing? I mean, I'm not using this to try to hook up with other girls. You believe me, right? And Greg's a nice guy. You like him, right?"

"I like him, Hudson," Zoey said. "I don't know. I just feel like I'm cheating on you."

"How can you be cheating if I'm right there? If you're doing what I'm telling you to do?"

Zoey gave a laugh. "Well, I do like that part," she admitted, grinning at her boyfriend. "I like it when you tell me what to do."

Hudson grinned back. "I know you do, you're my little submissive slut," he teased. They smiled into each other's eyes.

"So, what else did you like about it?" Hudson asked. "Come on, don't hold back. Tell me."

"Well ...," Zoey began. She laughed and her cheeks reddened. "This is embarrassing."

"Come on, this is me," Hudson said soothingly. "You can tell me anything."

"Well, okay," Zoey said. She hesitantly said, "You know that part, about Greg using me for his needs? That kinda got me hot."

Hudson smiled. He said, "I thought it did. It got me hot too." He kissed her, and then pulled his frat t-shirt over her head. She was naked except for panties and white cotton socks (she always wore socks to bed because her feet got cold at night).

Hudson cupped her small perky high school breasts, then ran his hands down her stomach. "Your body's so tight and sexy," he said lustfully. "I see guys – I see my friends – checking you out. I used to get pissed, but now I think about them getting hot looking at you. I think about them using your body for their needs."

Zoey giggled. "Hudson, you are a *Bad Boy*," she teased with a grin.

"But you like it too. You just said it," Hudson reminded her. "You like the idea of dudes using your body for their needs."

"I like … you *ordering* me to let them use my body for their needs," Zoey said hesitantly. They looked at each other for a moment. Then they were all over each other. Hudson was quickly inside her.

"Greg … he wants you again," Hudson panted as he fucked Zoey missionary. "He needs you to take care of his needs. We talked about it."

"Ohhh gawd," Zoey moaned. "You freaking *talked* about it?" she asked incredulously. She was panting as Hudson slid in and out of her. "He really said that?"

"He needs your body for his needs baby," Hudson said lustfully. "He told me this a few weeks ago. He probably needs you even more now."

"Gawd Hudson," she moaned again. "I don't … I don't get …" she sputtered, finding it hard to talk while they fucked. "He's cute. He should be able to get girls."

"He tries. No luck," Hudson said. Then he asked, "You think he's cute?"

"I mean, not like you, he's not super gorgeous like you," Zoey said immediately. "I'm just saying, Greg's not ugly."

"I think he's too passive. Girls don't like that," Hudson said. He found it exciting to talk about Greg as they had sex. He had to concentrate though and force himself not to cum too fast while thinking about Zoey and Greg together. Only losers came too fast. He didn't want Zoey to think less of him.

"I guess …," Zoey said noncommittally.

"Or maybe they just don't know how big a dick he has," Hudson joked with a grin. "Can you believe he has such a big horse cock?"

Without thinking, Zoey said, "God no. He's freaking huge."

Then she realized what she said. She didn't want to hurt her boyfriend's feelings. "But, I mean, size doesn't really matter," she quickly added.

As she said this, though, she remembered what Greg's condom package said. Magnum. Extra Large. And she remembered how his cock had felt so big – huge – inside her. How he had stretched her so much.

"It's okay Zoe baby," Hudson said as he kissed her. "You don't have to worry about hurting my feelings. I'm not worried about Greg. I know he's not your type."

Zoey looked into her boyfriend's eyes and said earnestly, "Hudson baby ... you're the *only* man who's my type." She kissed him back.

"I'm just saying ...," Hudson said, finding it hard to talk. Talking about Greg with Zoey was making him dizzy with lust. "I know his dick's bigger than mine. It doesn't bother me. I think it's hot actually."

Zoey's eyes got big. "Really? Seriously?" she asked with surprise.

"Yeah ... I can't explain why," Hudson said, looking lustful but unsure.

Zoey was surprised but also charmed by his show of indecision and vulnerability. She reached up and hugged him, and they kissed.

"That was really hot," Hudson said after they were done. He lay next to her now, both of them panting. He took off the condom and threw it away in a couple of tissues.

"Yeah," Zoey agreed with a giggle.

Hudson rolled over to her. He reached out and cupped one of her breasts. "I think it gets you hot talking about Greg," he said with a grin.

"I don't mind talking about it," Zoey said.

"So baby, are you going to let Greg use your body again to take care of his needs?" Hudson asked.

Zoey sucked in her breath. "God Hudson, you're incorrigible," she said.

Hudson moved his hand to her pussy. He knew she hadn't cum yet. She never did from intercourse alone.

"Don't deny it," he said as he began to touch her the way he knew she liked. "You just told me it gets you hot – Greg using your body to get off."

Zoey arched her back at the touch of her boyfriend's fingers on her clit. "The fantasy gets me hot," she said.

"This isn't just fantasy babe," Hudson said. "He's already fucked you twice."

Zoey sucked in her breath again. "Hudson baby ...," she began. "I'll always do what you want me to do. You know that. But I'm just afraid you'll get mad at me, and it'll hurt our relationship."

"That'll never happen Zoe baby," Hudson assured her.

Zoey hesitated. Then she decided to tell him. "What if I told you Greg almost made me cum last time?" she asked.

Hudson looked shocked. "Seriously?" he asked. "While you were fucking?"

Zoey nodded. "I think so. I'm not sure. You told him to pull out, remember? But I think I was about to cum."

"Wow," Hudson said incredulously. He stopped playing with Zoey's pussy and rolled onto his back. "Wow," he said again as he looked up at the ceiling.

His reaction instantly worried Zoey. She rolled to him and hugged him. "You see?" she said. "Now you're mad at me."

"I'm not mad ...," Hudson said. "I just need to think about this ...."

They were silent for long moments. The entire time, Zoey clung to Hudson, afraid he was mad at her.

Finally, Hudson said "I think it would be good."

"What?" Zoey asked, getting up on her elbow to look into his handsome face.

"I think it would be good if Greg made you cum," Hudson said, looking into Zoey's eyes. "I love you. I want you to experience that."

Zoey's lips parted and her eyes opened wide with surprise. "Are you serious?" she asked incredulously.

"I love you Zoey," Hudson said. "I want you to have everything."

Zoey's heart melted. At that moment, she loved Hudson more than ever.

She shook her head though. "Now that I know it's possible, I want to do it with you," she said. "Greg ... we have those memories with him. We can talk about it and get each other hot. But I think 2 times is enough. It's probably 2 times too much."

Hudson rolled onto Zoey so now he was on top. He was hard again, and Zoey felt his erection against her thigh.

"Hudson, god, really?" she said with a giggle. He hardly ever got hard again that fast.

"Yeah, I know," he said with a grin as he rolled on another condom. He pushed back into her pussy. "I don't know why ... but the idea of Greg fucking you and making you cum gets me hot."

Zoey's eyes opened wide with surprise again. Hudson was really surprising her tonight.

"I'm so hot, I won't last long," Hudson warned her. "Play with yourself baby. I want you to cum too."

Zoey nodded. She reached down between their bodies and began circling and stroking her clit as Hudson fucked her. They did this often. Even though she had never cum solely from intercourse, Zoey got her share of orgasms from Hudson's tongue, his fingers, and her own fingers.

They looked into each other's eyes and panted into each other's faces as they both worked themselves to orgasm.

CHAPTER 5

Where Hudson and Greg worked, Camilla was one of the most powerful partners. In addition to being a major rainmaker, she chaired the partnership committee. In that role, she had more influence than anyone on who became partner, and who didn't.

Camilla was married to Maynard, a professor of drama and theatre arts at Fordham University. While tenured, his income was small compared to Camilla's. Camilla was the breadwinner in their marriage, affording them the Central Park penthouse, oceanfront condo in South Beach, expensive wine collection, chauffeured BMWs, and the other trappings of their luxurious lifestyle.

Maynard was Camilla's age, mid-40s. They met young and had been married almost 20 years. They had two children, both in Ivy League colleges.

Maynard was very handsome in a dapper, college professor kind of way. No one would call Maynard ruggedly handsome. Nothing about Maynard was *rugged*. Instead, her husband was an elegant pretty boy. Camilla was fine with that, as elegant pretty boys were her thing.

And Maynard was blessed with an impressive manhood. Camilla had been surprised by his size the first time they had sex, because in her experience, pretty boys like Maynard with their fit yet slim bodies and refined yet smallish hands were below average in the manhood department. But not Maynard. He was a shortish, slim pretty boy with a big cock.

Camilla fell for Maynard because of his refined air, pretty face, fit body and large penis. Not necessarily in that order. She was more attracted to him now than ever before.

At 45, Camilla was still attractive and a head turner. She was curvy with big breasts and long legs. But she knew her best days were behind her. Unlike men, women didn't age well. She loved her two children, but two pregnancies and breast feeding had ravaged her body.

Camilla was able to hold onto her looks because she had the best of everything money could buy—makeup, hair stylists, personal trainers, dieticians, Botox, fashionable clothes ... everything a middle-aged women needed to stay attractive and desirable to men.

But she knew her looks and desirability were fading with each passing year, while her husband Maynard was only getting more handsome and more desirable.

Camilla's relationship with Maynard was complicated. He was handsome and charming and was around pretty, young coeds every day. Ripe girls at the height of their beauty and desirability. Since he taught drama and theatre arts, girls like that tended to flock to his classes. And to his private office hours.

Camilla knew Maynard cheated on her. She found out early on. She could divorce him but never would. She loved Maynard. She lusted for him too. And she knew Maynard would never leave her for a younger girl, because he needed her income to live his lavish and affluent lifestyle.

And, while Maynard had a taste for young flesh, Camilla had desires too.

So, years ago, Camilla and Maynard came to an agreement. This agreement saved their marriage. But also made their relationship complicated.

———◉———

CAMILLA WAS IN HER hotel room on one of her frequent business trips. Her skirt was pulled up around her waist and her legs were spread wide. She was looking at the top of the head of the man going down on her.

He was a boy, really, barely 20 years old. Like her husband, Camilla liked them young.

She had met the boy – Austin was his name – at a bar close to the local college. Camilla hunted at such bars when she was in the mood for barely legal meat.

Austin had a good tongue, especially given his youth. Camilla was breathing hard in her expensive Fendi dress. She could tell the young college student was into legs. He caressed her stockinged legs and ran his fingertips over the stilettos of her Jimmy Choo high heels as he ate her out.

Camilla rolled her head back and moaned as she orgasmed on Austin's tongue. It was a good orgasm. It would satiate her until she was back home with Maynard.

Camilla put her high heeled foot on Austin's shoulder and pushed him away. He grinned and wiped his mouth with his sleeve as he stood up.

Camilla looked at his face. He was very handsome. A pretty boy. Just her type.

"Take off your clothes," she said.

Austin's grin grew bigger. He was fine with being ordered around. She was an older bitch after all. And he could tell she was successful, by her expensive clothes and the opulence of her hotel room. Maybe he might even get a summer internship out of it.

Camilla watched as Austin stripped. He was slim and not too tall. Just like Maynard. That's why she had picked him.

His penis was small. It didn't surprise Camilla. With his slim stature and small hands, she'd assumed the boy would be small. Her husband Maynard was an exception, and she knew from personal experience that he was a rare exception.

"Get on your back," Camilla ordered.

As Austin got onto the bed, Camilla pulled off her dress. Austin's eyes were on her sexily lingeried body.

Camilla straddled Austin's hips. She wasn't wearing panties. She never did when she planned to fuck. And she woke up this morning knowing he was going to seduce a boy like Austin after her meetings were done, and bring him to here to her hotel room.

Camilla lowered herself onto Austin's cock. She felt him inside her, but he certainly didn't stretch her. Her pussy used to be tight, but that was before giving birth 2 times. She loved her 2 boys, but she mourned the loss of her tight pussy. Her body was never the same after two pregnancies. Maybe if her face and body were still perfect like they had been when she was 25, Maynard's eyes wouldn't wander so much.

Camilla moved up and down on Austin's cock. His penis was only about 5 inches long and thin, but she knew how to position herself to achieve orgasm. And his pretty face and slim, tight body got her hot. She liked looking down at him as she fucked him.

Austin reached up and fondled her big tits. She let him. She liked when men touched her breasts. She wouldn't let Austin kiss her though. She only ever kissed her husband Maynard.

CHAPTER 6

Soon after joining his firm, the first thing Hudson noticed about Camilla was she wore stiletto high heels every day. And she usually wore hose rather than going bare leg like most girls nowadays. He admired Camilla for that. Hudson hoped Zoey would still be wearing stockings and high heels when she was in her forties.

Hudson also learned fast – like all his peers – that Camilla was a balls buster with no patience for fools. She was probably the most powerful person in their firm. If she didn't like you, you had no chance of making partner.

Hudson rarely saw Camilla. Her kingdom was the penthouse floor where all the C-level players spent their time. Even *they* were afraid of Camilla. Everyone called her the Dragon Lady.

So, there was a sense of trepidation when Hudson saw her walk into Greg's office. Was Camilla giving Greg the bad news everyone expected? It was Friday. It was so like Camilla to ruin Greg's weekend.

Then he was shocked when Camilla walked into his office an hour later. She sat in the chair in front of his desk and crossed her long, stockings clad legs.

Camilla stared at Hudson for long moments. Then she got to the point. "Hudson, you've impressed me," she said. "I'm starting a new biz dev project. Very high profile. Very high ceiling. I need a lead assistant. I want you to be my assistant."

Hudson's eyes went wide. This was big. *Big*. Not only would it guarantee his seat at the partnership table, it would also fast track him to coveted leadership positions. It was such a big opportunity he ignored being called an "assistant."

"I'm in Camilla," Hudson said immediately.

"This project will involve serious travel," Camilla told him. "Sometimes overnights. Sometimes weekend trips."

"I'm in," Hudson assured her. "I'm up for it."

Camilla nodded her head, sealing their new collaboration. She looked at his face for another long moment. It unnerved Hudson. He was a good-looking guy and was used to girls looking at him. But the Dragon Lady?

FRIDAY MEANT HAPPY hour. Zoey met Hudson at the bar. She was ecstatic when he told her about the new project with Camilla.

Then they found out Camilla had given Greg official notice he wasn't on partnership track. Since their company was up or out, he would have to leave. But Camilla did give Greg some time to find a new job.

They were surprised Greg was at the happy hour. He put on a brave face and said he needed to get drunk.

Most of their co-workers didn't care about Greg. He wasn't part of their group. He was too different, and people had problems dealing with different. If anything, they said Wall Street wasn't for him, so it was good he was leaving so he could find a job that suit him better.

But Hudson and Zoey cared. They liked Greg. They were friends. They stayed with Greg throughout the happy hour, so he wouldn't be alone, and tried to make him feel better.

As the happy hour wound down and their co-workers dispersed, Hudson pulled Zoey aside so they could speak privately. "It really sucks about Greg," he said.

"Yeah, it really does," Zoey agreed. "I wish we could make him feel better."

"You know what he needs to feel better?"

"What?" Zoey asked.

Hudson looked into his girlfriend's eyes and said, "He needs to feel like a man."

Zoey stared back at Hudson.

Still looking into her eyes, he said, "Every guy deserves to feel like a man sometimes. Especially when you're kicked in the gut like this."

"Hudson, you're freaking crazy," Zoey lamented under her breath. "You just got a promotion –."

"It's not a promotion," Hudson corrected her.

"It's practically a promotion!" Zoey said with exasperation. "I want to celebrate with *you*."

"And I want *you* to make Greg feel like a man," Hudson said. Then looking into her eyes again, he added, "I want my girlfriend to take care of Greg's needs."

"Hudson ...," Zoey said, shaking her head. "God ..."

"I want you to go to his apartment," Hudson continued. "If you're alone with him, he'll feel more like a man. And, if I'm not there, maybe it'll be easier for you to cum."

Zoey stared at Hudson. She couldn't believe what he was saying. "You really want him to do that to me?" she asked incredulously.

"I want you to experience it," Hudson said. "I love you. I want to give this to you."

"Aren't you jealous?" Zoey asked.

"Yeeees!" Hudson hissed. "It's driving me insane! But I don't know. Maybe because it's his big cock. Maybe because he's taller. The angle. The leverage. I don't know. All I know is, if he can do this for you, something I can't do ... then I want this for you. I want you to experience it. And I admit, this turns me on. I can't stop thinking about it."

Zoey stared at her boyfriend.

"Remember last time?" Hudson asked. "After Greg left. And we were making love?"

Zoey nodded.

"You felt so loose. His big dick really stretched you out," Hudson said. "I want to feel that again. You want to celebrate with me? That's how I want to celebrate."

"Hudson ... god," she softly whispered.

"So, it's a win-win for all of us." Hudson said with a grin.

"I guess ...," she said, her voice trailing away.

Hudson smiled at her agreement (albeit her reluctant agreement). "Let's go get Greg," he said brightly. "I know he'll be up for it. We can't let people see you leaving alone with him. We'll walk a couple blocks. Then you and Greg can get an uBer to his place, and I'll meet you back home at the loft apartment.

———⊙———

ZOEY WAS IN GREG'S apartment, looking at the pictures on the shelves. She'd never been in his apartment before. It was much smaller than Hudson's. And Greg didn't own it, he rented.

"This is your family?" she asked.

Greg moved closer so he was behind her. "Yes. That's my mom and dad," he said, pointing to the pictures. "That's my sister. And my two brothers."

"Wow. Four kids. A big family."

"How big is your family?"

"Well, you know, my mom and dad," Zoey said. "And I have an older sister."

"Oh, okay," Greg said. He wasn't interested really in Zoey's family, not at that moment. He moved closer to her. He pulled her long blonde hair to the side and kissed her neck.

Zoey's body tensed and she took a step away. "Sorry," she said. "I haven't been alone with a man since I started dating Hudson. I mean, alone like this."

"I get it," Greg said, giving her a reassuring smile and moving a respectful distance away.

"Do you have anything to drink?" she asked him.

"Uh, sure," Greg said.

When Zoey saw him pull a bottle of wine from a shelf, she said "Do you have anything stronger?"

"Ah ...," Greg said as he pulled down 2 bottles. One was Grey Goose vodka, and the other was Bombay gin.

Zoey said, "I'll take the vodka."

"You take it dirty?" Greg asked. He'd heard Hudson order her drink many times. "I don't think I have any olives."

"That's okay. Just a shot ...."

Greg poured 2 shot glasses. He gave her one. They clinked glasses, then they both gulped the vodka.

Then they stood there, looking awkward at each other. Zoey gave a nervous laugh. Then she took Greg's hand. "Come on," she said, leading him to his sofa. "Or, ah ..." she said, looking down the hall.

Greg understood what she was thinking. "I think my bed's more comfortable," he said. Then he laughed nervously and said, "This is embarrassing."

"Yeah," Zoey said with a laugh back.

Greg took Zoey's hand and led her to his bedroom. He turned on the light.

Zoey looked around. His bedroom was simple but neat. A double bed, a side table with an Ikea lamp. A lot of bookcases.

Then it hit her. *I'm in another man's bedroom,* she thought. *Wow. Wow ....*

Greg looked unsure at the light switch. Then he asked Zoey, "Lights on or off?"

"Would it be terrible if I said off?" Zoey asked.

"No, of course," Greg hurriedly said. He turned off the light. It was still enough light to see, though, from the moonlight coming in through the window.

Greg led Zoey to his bed. They sat on the edge of the bed. She touched the bed. "You make your bed every day?" she asked.

"Yeah. I mean, what else would you do?"

"Ha," Zoey laughed. "I don't think Hudson even knows how to make a bed." She smiled at Greg and said, "That's kinda cute. What you just said."

Greg smiled back. Then they leaned towards each other and kissed.

———— ◆ ————

HUDSON WAS AT HOME, in the loft apartment. He had his cock out and was stroking himself as he imagined what they were doing. What Greg was doing to Zoey. What he was doing to the girl he loved.

He had never been so excited in his life. Zoey was alone with another man. What was Greg doing to her? Licking her ass? Her pussy? Fondling her breasts? Fucking her? Hudson grimaced even as he pleasured himself with his hand. The jealousy tore at his insides. It hurt. Yet it felt so good!

Was he kissing her? Was Zoey kissing him back? God, the thought of them kissing hurt the most. He didn't understand why. Why does Greg kissing Zoey make him more jealous than him fucking her? But it did. It was 100 times worse. Or better. It got him so hot! Hudson imagined them kissing, and then his cock exploded, his orgasm so strong jets of his cum hit his chest, almost up to his neck.

And then something happened that was unexpected. The jealousy, the hurt, the angst – they hit him like a ton of bricks! The feeling was debilitating. He couldn't move, he couldn't breathe.

Zoey was with Greg. She was alone with him!

Then he remembered ... Greg was going to make Zoey cum! With just his cock! Greg was going to make Zoey cum from intercourse, for the first time in her life!

Hudson hunched over at the waist, the wave of angst so powerful, so hurtful. It was like a knife in his chest. And then something else unexpected happened. Something amazing.

His cock was hard again. So was his lust. And so was his desire for Greg to use Zoey's body to take care of his needs.

———⬤———

THEIR KISS STARTED soft. Tentative. Then a little harder, a little more urgent. And then Zoey opened her lips, and Greg eased in his tongue. She met his tongue with her own, and then she pushed her tongue into his mouth.

They kissed for long moments. When they pulled away, they were both panting. "Wow," Greg said between pants.

"Yeah, wow," Zoey said, breathing just as hard as him. It surprised her. Greg was a good kisser.

She reached for the Grey Goose and poured 2 more shots. "You want one?" she asked.

But before she could drink her shot, Greg pushed her hair to the side and began kissing up her neck. "Oh ah, Greg, Greg honey …," she gasped. Then she gave into it and rolled her head back, exposing her sensitive neck to his hungry lips and tongue.

As Greg kissed up her neck, to just below her ear, she moaned "Ahhh ahhh ahhh …."

As he kissed and nibbled just below her ear, he put his hand over her breast. He cupped and fondled her through her dress. "Is this okay?" he whispered. "Can I touch you here?"

"Yeah, yeah …" she moaned, arching her back so her tits pressed against his palm. "Greg… you don't have to ask me. Just … just do it."

Greg pulled away and stared at her for a long moment, processing what she just said.. Then he was frantically unbuttoning her dress (it buttoned up the front). When it was unbuttoned down to her waist, he forced a hand in. He flipped up her bra. Then he grabbed one of her bare breasts, squeezing it hard, finding her nipple and pinching it between his thumb and forefinger.

"Ohhhhhhhh ....," Zoey whined, grimacing at the pain. At the pleasure.

Greg's movements were rushed and unpolished. But she was glad he was taking control.

Greg reached down and jerked up her dress. He pulled it up to her belly button, so she was completely exposed from her waist down. He pulled out his cock and quickly rolled on a condom. Jerking her thong to the side, he pushed into her. He penetrated her pussy. Then he fucked her.

———◉———

WHEN GREG WAS DONE, Zoey gently said "Greg ... can you get off?"

"Oh sorry," he said, moving to pull out.

He moved fast so she warned, "Careful okay?" She didn't want the condom to fall off when he pulled out.

"Oh yeah, sorry," Greg apologized again. He held the condom at the base of his cock as he slowly pulled out.

"Wow, wow," Zoey said under her breath as he slowly pulled out of her. His thickness – his length – felt freaking amazing as he slowly pulled out, even though he was softening.

"Sorry I was rough," Greg said sheepishly. "I guess I was pissed at Camilla and took it out on you."

"Ha," Zoey laughed. She joked, "Oh thanks a lot. The Dragon Lady screws you over and I pay for it." Then she realized what she said. Looking down at her feet, she said, "Sorry. I shouldn't have said that. I was joking."

"What? That Camilla screwed me over? She did. Actually, I came out ahead as I got to be with you again."

Zoey looked down at her feet. She was smiling though. She said "Greg ... don't be so sweet, okay?"

He looked at her like he didn't understand. Still smiling, she tenderly ran her hand along his cheek.

Then her expression got serious. She fixed her bra and dress to cover herself, then said, "I've got to call Hudson." She grabbed her phone and went into Greg's kitchen, leaving him in the bedroom.

"Hey you. Are you okay?" she said when Hudson answered.

"How is it going?" Hudson asked excitedly.

"We're done," Zoey said. "I'm coming home."

"Done?" Hudson said with surprise. He looked at the clock. "You haven't even been there an hour."

"I know, but ... he didn't need much time."

Her words resonated in Hudson's head, like fireworks. "So ... he fucked you?" he asked excitedly.

"Yes."

"Wow, god, wow Zoey," Hudson moaned over the phone. "Zoe baby, say he fucked you. Say the words."

Zoey hesitated, then said "Greg fucked me."

"God Zoey," Hudson moaned, bending over at the waist as pain and pleasure both punched him in the gut.

"He couldn't keep his hands off you?" Hudson asked. "He used your hot body?"

"Yeah baby," Zoey told her boyfriend. "It was like he was crazy. We were kissing, and then all of a sudden, he threw me onto his bed."

"You did it on his bed?!" Hudson groaned. His girlfriend was in another man's bed!

"Zoe baby, you kissed him?" he asked excitedly.

"Yeah," she said.

"You made out with him?"

"Yeah."

"Say it Zoey," Hudson urged. "Say the words."

"I made out with Greg," Zoey said. Then she added, "He's a good kisser."

"Oh god, fuck, oh god, Zoey, so good, so good, Zoey ...," Hudson moaned into the phone. He felt the big vise squeezing his heart, the intense jealousy tearing at his gut. Still, it felt so delicious! So exhilarating!

"Zoe baby ... you're doing so good baby," he said excitedly. "So fucking good."

"This really excites you?" Zoey asked.

"Oh god yessss!" Hudson hissed. "My cock is fucking steel! I'm stroking myself! I've already cum twice!"

"Wow," Zoey said with amazement. She was still getting her head around how much this excited her boyfriend.

"He used a condom though, right?"

"Yes. I made sure it didn't fall off when he pulled out."

"Oh gawd," Hudson groaned. Hearing her talk about sex with another man was so arousing. "You like feeling his big cock inside you?"

"Honestly, it happened so fast ...," Zoey said.

"That's because he needed you baby," Hudson gushed excitedly. "He needed your tight sexy body to take care of his needs. And I gave you to him baby. I gave him your pussy. He can do anything he wants with your body."

Zoey found herself breathing hard as his words pushed her sub-space buttons. "Hudson ...," she said, her voice getting husky. "Tell me what you want me to do."

"How many times has he fucked you?" Hudson asked.

"Just once," Zoey answered. Then she asked, "Is that enough to make Greg feel like a man?"

"No, not nearly enough. He's probably hard again, needing you," Hudson said. He was breathing hard as he stroked his cock. "I want you to take care of him baby. I want you to let him use you."

Zoey sucked in her breath. Her head was spinning.

"What are you wearing?"

"My dress."

"Take it off baby. Strip baby, let him see your tight sexy body. You know that scene in *Wolf of Wallstreet*, the one with Margot Robbie? Go to Greg like that. In just stockings and heels. Then let him do whatever he wants to you."

"Hudson, god ... this is getting me so hot," Zoey moaned. "But aren't you jealous?"

"I *am* jealous, this is killing me!" Hudson exclaimed. "But I want him to use you. Until he feels like a man. He can use your body until he feels like a man. Has he made you cum yet?"

"No. I'm not sure it'll happen."

"I want you to try," Hudson urged her. "Don't worry about me. I want you to try. Let Greg make you cum."

"You love me though, right Hudson?" Zoey asked, needing assurance. "Even if he makes me cum, you'll still love me right?"

"Zoey honey, Zoe baby, I'll always love you," Hudson assured her. "Now go back to Greg. Be his little submissive slut."

———————⊙———————

ZOEY TOOK OFF HER DRESS, bra and thong panties. She was left in just thigh high stockings and high heels. She ran her fingers through her hair and brushed on new lipstick. She look at herself in the mirror. She did sorta look like Margot Robbie in that movie scene.

She went back into Greg's bedroom. As she entered, she turned on the light. Hudson told her to let Greg see her. So, she turned on the light.

Greg was waiting for her, looking at her as she entered. His back was against the headboard, and he had put his boxers back on.

"God Zoey," Greg moaned as he looked at Zoey's hot bod. "Your body's so amazing! You're so perfect!"

Zoey smiled. She sat on the edge of the bed and looked at Greg.

"Sorry I was rough," Greg said.

"It's okay," Zoey said.

"Sorry, I should get you something else to drink," Greg said, moving to get out of the bed to go to the kitchen.

Zoey stopped him with a hand to his thigh. "It's okay Greg, I don't want anything," she said. She began to caress his thigh with the pads of her fingers. "So, Hudson says you haven't been with a girl for a while."

Greg looked embarrassed. "You probably think I'm a loser," he said.

"I do not," Zoey assured him with a soft voice. "I think you're nice. I think you're cute." She moved her hand up his leg as she said, "I think you have a nice body."

Greg gulped. He was hard again, and his hard-on bulged out his boxers. Zoey stared at his erection for long moments.

Then Zoey stood up. She posed for Greg, the way Margot posed for Leonardo DiCaprio in the movie. She asked with a husky voice, "Do you still need my body, Greg?"

Greg looked like he was going to have a heart attack. He was practically salivating. He said, "I can't believe ...." His voice trailed off.

"You can't believe what?" she asked.

"I guess ...," Greg hesitantly began. He looked embarrassed. "I've always thought you're hot. I can't believe what we've done ... that you're here. I guess I've had a thing for you. I know that's shitty since Hudson's my friend."

Zoey smiled at him. "It's not shitty Greg," she assured him. "People have harmless crushes all the time. I'm really flattered. And I've noticed you too. I think you're really nice. And I told you I think you're cute."

Greg smiled like she had just made his day ... his year.

"Slide over here Greg," Zoey said, motioning to the edge of the bed. Greg moved so he was sitting on the edge of the bed.

"Why don't you open your legs?" she said. Zoey wasn't used to this. She wasn't a seductress. That wasn't her personality. She preferred the man to be in control. To control her. But she knew Greg – shy, timid Greg – needed some direction.

Greg spread his legs. Zoey bunched up her hair in her hands, giving Greg a sweet smile as she stepped inside his open legs.

Zoey teasingly let her hair drop as she got onto her knees. Greg sucked in his breath. "Oh god," he groaned, anticipating what she was going to do.

Greg was fully hard, and he was so long his cock extended beyond the waistband of his boxers. Zoey put her hands on his crotch, and used her index fingers to trace the outline that was formed in his shorts. Her eyes were on the head and the part of his shaft that extended beyond the waistband. When her fingers reached it, she said "Greg ... this is really impressive."

She looked at him and smiled. Then she leaned over and softly licked the exposed cockhead and shaft. "Oh shit!" Greg moaned, his body tensing up at the feel of her tongue.

Zoey felt him tense up. She rubbed his thighs and said "Calm down honey. This is all for you."

"Thank you, thank you!" Greg gushed. Zoey smiled into his eyes.

Zoey curled her fingers into the waistband of Greg's boxers and pulled them down. His big cock popped up so it stood straight up.

"Wow," Zoey said as she looked at it. She'd been with him two times already, but this was the first time she'd really been able to look at his penis.

His cock was like a tower, broader at the base and then tapering somewhat to the head, which was like a mushroom. There were veins that ran up the sides, and then a really big vein running up the underside. The skin was smooth and soft, and somewhat pinkish.

Zoey saw he had big balls, but the ball sack was really tight. He had pubic hair. This differed from Hudson who kept himself completely hairless like a porn star, which she thought was very sexy.

Of course, the other difference between Greg and her boyfriend was the size of their penises. Hudson was a nice size, she had no complaints. She measured him once. When he was hard, Hudson was a little less than 5 inches long, and a little bigger than 3 inches around.

She looked it up on the internet. Hudson's penis was smaller than average. But she had no complaints, as he was a very skilled and experienced lover. Also, she loved looking into his face when they made love. Hudson was the most handsome man she'd ever seen. Having sex with such a beautiful man was a major turn-on.

And Hudson was a bad boy too. And he was dominant, a top, a *Real Man*. Zoey was very happy with their sex life.

But still, she was impressed with Greg's size. And very curious. She put her hands around it.

Wow. Even with one hand on top of the other, there was still more cock. And, her fingers couldn't close around it. There was a gap of at least an inch.

"Greg, geez, how freaking big are you?" she asked. "Have you ever measured yourself?"

Greg shook his head no. Although he wasn't really able to focus on her question. He was still getting his head around Zoey – Hudson's beautiful girlfriend! – on her knees between his legs and holding his cock.

Zoey was amazed by his size, both the length and girth. It was easily the biggest cock she'd ever seen, and certainly the biggest she'd ever held in her hands. She couldn't believe she'd been able to fit this monster inside her. Yet he'd already been inside her three times!

What also amazed her – and something she'd never appreciated or ever really thought about – was how solid it felt. And how heavy it was. "Greg ... geez. How do you even get this thing into your pants?"

"Zoey ...," Greg moaned. "You're driving me crazy."

Zoey's lips parted in surprise. She realized she was teasing the poor boy. She licked her palms to lubricate them, then she wrapped her hands around his shaft again. She began pumping him up and down. "Better?" she asked.

Greg eagerly nodded. He timidly asked, "Zoey ... can you put it in your mouth, like you did that first time?"

Zoey gave him a weak smile. "Greg, can I tell you something?" she said gently. "Don't ask so much. Don't apologize. You're the man. I'm the girl. You tell me what to do."

Greg didn't seem to understand or know what to do.

Zoey gave him a friendly, encouraging smile. Then she took one of his hands. She guided his hand to the back of her head. "Greg, grab my hair. Pull me to your cock," she said.

Greg hesitated. Then he curled his fingers into Zoey's hair. He pulled her to his cock.

Zoey resisted. "Pull harder," she urged Greg. "Don't worry about hurting me."

Greg pulled harder. Zoey resisted more, then allowed him to pull her head to his crotch.

She swirled her tongue around his big cockhead. Then she took him into her mouth. Soon she was bobbing up and down, her hands moving up and down in sync with her mouth.

Greg had both his hands behind her head. Unlike most men though, he wasn't pushing her down his shaft. Instead, he allowed her to control things. Zoey wished he would be more aggressive and force his cock down her throat and make her gag. But she knew it wasn't Greg's personality.

"God, god, god ..." Greg groaned. Zoey sensed he was close to cumming. She pulled her mouth off his cock. He looked at her lips. They were slick with his pre-cum and her saliva. He got even more aroused at the sight.

Zoey stroked Greg's shaft with her hands. Looking into his eyes, she said "I want you to cum in my mouth." Then she ran his cockhead across her cheek and asked, "Or do you want to cum on my face?"

"Which one Greg?" she teasingly asked.

Greg seemed to freeze. He didn't know how to answer.

Zoey reached under him and cupped his big, heavy balls. With a grin she said, "I bet you have enough cum in here to do both." Greg groaned.

Then Zoey took him into her mouth again and worked her magic. She was good at giving head. She really worked at it. The way she looked at it, it was her job to give her man pleasure. Greg was the biggest she had ever had in her mouth (or her hands) by far, and she probably wasn't as good with him as she was with Hudson, but still his constant moaning told her she was doing a good job.

In a few moments, Greg was cumming. Two powerful jets of his semen hit the back of her throat. Her cheeks ballooned as it filled her mouth, and she worked to swallow it. Greg came more into her mouth.

When she thought he was about done, she took him out of her mouth and pointed his cockhead at her face. She thought he might dribble a little on her cheek. But instead, 3 more powerful jets of his sperm hit her face. The sperm splashed her cheeks, her nose, a little got into her eyes, and some got into her hair. When he was finally done, Zoey's pretty face was soaked in Greg's jizz.

"Wow," Zoey gasped, amazed at how much he had cum. "Wow."

She looked up at Greg and said, "Greg, look what you did to me."

Greg moaned at the sight, and his cock began hardening again.

Zoey stared at his hardening cock. Feeling amazed, she said under her breath, "Holy shit."

AFTER CLEANING UP IN the bathroom, Zoey got back into bed with Greg. She had taken off her remaining lingerie, so now she was completely naked. She got under the covers. Even though she had now had sex with Greg 3 times (4 counting the blowjob), she still didn't feel comfortable being naked with him.

Greg felt the same way. He had put his boxers back on, along with a t-shirt.

"I thought you were getting ready to leave," Greg said.

"Oh. Do you have something to do? I can leave," Zoey said.

"No, no," Greg quickly said. "I just thought you wanted to get home to Hudson."

"Hudson told me to stay until I've taken care of your needs," Zoey said. "Do you still have needs Greg?"

Greg looked embarrassed. "I guess I do," he said sheepishly.

Zoey looked at his crotch. His boxers were already straining with his hardening cock. "I guess you do too," she said with a grin and giggle. "But let's just hang for a minute." She looked around his bedroom. There were bookcases everywhere, stuffed with books. It was the same way in his living room. He even stored books on top of the cabinets in the kitchen.

"You really like to read," Zoey said as she looked around the room.

"I love books," Greg said enthusiastically. "Most of them are used. You know, from used bookstores."

"Wouldn't you rather have new books?" Zoey asked.

"I like old books," Greg said. He picked up the book on his nightstand. It was *"Foundation"* by Isaac Asimov. He said, "I like thinking about all the people who have read this book. You know. This particular copy of this novel."

"Yeah, I can see how that's cool," Zoey said. "So ... real bookstores still exist? I used to go to a Barnes & Noble, but it closed a long time ago. I thought everyone bought them from Amazon."

"Most are out of business," Greg lamented, looking sad. "But one of the best used bookstores is downstairs. Did you see it? Java Books. That's how I got this apartment. I've bought so many books there, the owner let me rent this space. It's right above the bookstore."

Zoey nodded. Greg's apartment was a walk-up. She'd seen a store as Greg opened the door to the staircase but didn't notice that it was a used bookstore. She actually thought it was a Starbucks or something since she smelled aromas of coffee and heard expresso machines frothing milk.

"So, can I ask you a personal question?" Zoey said. "I guess I don't get why you have trouble getting girls. You're cute. You're nice. You've got a good job. And, well, you've got that." Zoey motioned to his crotch.

"I won't have my job much longer," Greg lamented. "The Dragon Lady gave me 2 months to find a new job."

"Don't think about that Greg," Zoey said encouragingly. "You're smart. You're young. You'll find a new job – a better job – really fast. Anyways, that just happened. It doesn't explain why you have trouble meeting girls."

Zoey's cheeks flushed with embarrassment as she added, "I mean, Greg, your penis is very impressive. A lot of girls are into that. You shouldn't have any problems getting girls to go out to you."

"How exactly do I let girls know about it? Take out an ad in the *New York Times*?" Greg joked.

"Have you ever been in a bar, and ever *'accidentally'* rubbed up against a girl?" Zoey asked. "Guys do that to me all the time."

"And that's enough to let you know how big it is?"

"It's enough," Zoey said, looking at his cock. It was fully hard, so it was extending past the waistband of his boxers again. "Trust me Greg. For you especially, it's enough." Zoey couldn't help giggling, and Greg joined in with a big grin.

"So, are you into that too?" Greg asked.

"Well, honestly, size has never been that important to me. But I have a lot of girlfriends who are size queens." Zoey was still looking at his hard-on. She reached out caressed the part of his cock that extended beyond his boxers. "But I admit, I'm curious about your big thing."

She looked into his face. She saw he was breathing harder. With a soft voice, she asked, "So ... you ready to go again?"

Greg eagerly nodded his head.

"Take off your t-shirt Greg," Zoey said. As she said this, she pushed her hand into his boxers and wrapped her hand around his cock. Greg hurriedly pulled his t-shirt over his head.

They leaned into each other and kissed. As they did, Zoey stroked his cock, and if anything it got even harder.

Greg reached into the blanket, hungry for Zoey's body. Zoey pushed the blanket off her.

Greg took a moment to gaze at her body. It was the first time he'd seen her completely naked. His eyes excitedly moved from her little, perfect breasts to her flat stomach, her long shapely legs, and even her pretty feet. Then his eyes focused on her pussy. He saw she was completely bare of hair, except for a small, trimmed landing strip above her clit.

"God," he said like he was awestruck.

"Kiss me Greg," Zoey said to him. Soon they were making out and fondling each other. After a few minutes, they were both ready.

"Greg honey," Zoey said between kisses. She was breathing hard. He was too. She asked, "Condom?"

Greg hurriedly rolled a condom onto his shaft. He got on top of Zoey, between her open legs.

"Okay?" he asked.

Zoey nodded. "Okay," she said. She mentally prepared herself to be penetrated and stretched. Her pussy was wet. She was definitely aroused, and she wanted Greg inside her. She still worried about how this might affect her relationship with Hudson. But Hudson's words had assured her, at least for the moment. She kept telling herself, *"Hudson wants me to do this."*

Greg pushed into her. Zoey groaned. Even though he'd already fucked her not too long ago, the way he stretched her still made her grimace.

"Oh fuck. Greg, you are seriously big," she gasped.

"I'll go slow," Greg promised. He pushed deeper in.

Soon he was fully inside her. It still took time. It wasn't like Hudson, who could get balls deep in Zoey almost immediately. But each time with Greg, it was getting easier. She was gradually getting used to his size.

Greg began moving in and out, going slow. With each stroke, he went deep, going all the way in, and then pulling all the way out. "Oh wow, oh wow, that feels good Greg, god, god, it feels really good," Zoey moaned as Greg slowly long stroked her.

"Yeah, yeah, you feel really good Zoey," Greg said as he looked down into Zoey's beautiful blue eyes. "You feel really tight."

"You ... you feel good ... you feel good too," Zoey said, looking back up into Greg's face. She struggled to speak as he fucked her. "Greg honey ... can you hold off?"

"I think so," Greg said, nodding. Zoey's pussy felt so incredibly good, but since he'd already cum twice, he wouldn't cum as fast this time.

Zoey thought about it. She could make Greg cum fast. She knew how to do that.

Or she could take it slow and try to cum.

She still felt like it would be betraying Hudson, to allow Greg to be the first man to ever make her cum through intercourse. She could prevent that. A little dirty talk. Cupping and scratching his balls with her nails. A finger caressing his crack, and then tickling his asshole. She knew how to make Greg cum fast.

Or Zoey could try to cum. She wanted to cum from intercourse.

She was 23. She'd lost her virginity on her 15th birthday (and it was actually legal because of local Romeo and Juliet laws). Eight years of penetration sex, and not once had she cum from it. She had never had a vaginal orgasm.

Her girlfriends talked about having "*mind blowing*" orgasms. And it always happened during intercourse. Girls never talked about having "*epic*" orgasms from getting fingered or eaten out. Once her girlfriend called it a "*life changing*" orgasm after a night of frenzied sex. It had been from fucking though. It was always from fucking.

It was *always* from cumming on a man's cock.

Zoey wanted to experience this. And Hudson *wanted her* to experience it. He was practically ordering her to do this. Her boyfriend's encouragement helped ease her concerns.

Also, if she managed to do it with Greg – if she found out it was really possible – then she might be able to do it with Hudson. She knew that could really send her sex life with Hudson to new levels.

"Greg honey, remember last time, you leaned forward?" Zoey asked as she looked up at him. "And, you like, dug your feet into the mattress? Do that again."

Greg nodded. He leaned forward on his elbows and leveraged his toes into the mattress. The combination caused his cock to rub upwards against Zoey's walls as he moved in and out.

Zoey closed her eyes at the sensations, saying, "Yeah, yeah, that's it ... now a little more. Yeah, like that, yeah, keep going ...."

Greg leaned forward more, digging his toes into the mattress for leverage, using his long legs to angle his cock upwards into Zoey's pussy.

"Oh fuck yeah, shit, yeah, shit, that's it, yeah, yeah, shit, shit, yeah, ...," Zoey panted. What Greg was doing, where he was rubbing her, it felt so good. Not now, but later, she would realize that he was rubbing against both her clit and her g-spot at the same time.

"I can feel your nipples ... they're hard ... I can feel them against my chest," Greg said, straining to speak as he moved in and out of her pussy.

"Yeah? Is that sexy Greg? Do you like it?" Zoey asked him.

"Yeah, I do, I do," Greg moaned. Both their cheeks were flushed from passion, they were breathing hard, and they were looking into each other's eyes as they spoke. "You feel so good Zoey ... you're so ... tight," he said, his nostrils flaring as he stroked in and out. He was big and she was tight, so it was an exertion to keep moving in and out of her.

"Don't cum yet Greg ...," Zoey warned.

"I won't, I won't," he promised. He closed his eyes and gritted his teeth, forcing himself to hold off despite the intense pleasure of Zoey's tight, silky pussy.

"Because, oh god ...," Zoey moaned, clenching her eyes shut. She felt it building inside her. "I think it might be happening ...."

"Are you cumming?" Greg asked.

Zoey opened her eyes and looked up at him. "Greg ... take my hands," she whimpered. "Hold them over my head."

Greg took her hands and pulled them above her head.

"Hold my hands there Greg," Zoey said pleadingly. "Hold my hands. Hold them tight. Don't let me move. And keep fucking me. Don't stop."

Zoey concentrated. She moved underneath Greg, adjusting herself to make the angle perfect.

"Oh god, oh god," Zoey whimpered. "Just like that, Greg. Keep fucking me, just like that. Keep going. A little harder Greg. Harder. Yeah ... yeah ... oh god ... shit ... shit ... oh god ...."

Greg had surprising stamina, pushing all the way in, all the way out (except for the head), then back in again, going balls deep, pumping her over and over, long stroking her that way, staying at the angle she wanted, and all the while pinning her wrists above her head.

It took a few minutes. Eventually, Zoey whimpered, "Oh my god, oh god ...."

She felt her body going over the edge. It was like a slow wave, getting bigger and bigger, then peaking, cresting. Her head rolled back with her eyes clenched closed. Her pretty manicured toes curled as she whimpered, "Oh shit, shit, I'm cumming, I'm cumming ...."

Then the orgasm slammed her, the wave crashing down hard! A *tidal* wave crashing down hard!

"Aaaaaaahhhhhhhhh gaaaaaaaaaawd...." Zoey screamed as the orgasm exploded inside her, her back arching as bolts of orgasmic pleasure shot through her body. She gripped Greg's hands so hard her nails almost drew blood.

Zoey needed one last thing to make it perfect. As intense orgasmic pleasure flooded her body, she screamed, "Kiss me, Greg! Kiss me!"

Still pinning her hands, still moving in and out at the same angle, Greg lowered his head and kissed Zoey. He kissed her through her orgasm. He tongued her through her orgasm. All the while, Zoey moaned into Greg's mouth.

And the orgasm seemed to go on forever. She had never experienced anything like it. When it finally ended, she was left incoherent, her body shuddering from aftershocks of her climax, and then feeling completely like jelly.

Greg let her hands go. He rubbed his palms to dull the pain of her clawing.

"Wow ... wow," she panted.

"Are you okay?" Greg asked. His body was still. He was holding himself up on his elbows and knees, his hard cock still halfway inside her.

Zoey opened her eyes. She saw Greg looking at her. She said, "That was amazing. Intense. Epic."

"You came?" he asked.

"Yeah, I came," she said dreamily. Then she laughed. With the laugh in her voice, she said, "God, that was so awesome." She wanted to say more, but she felt like she shouldn't. Especially since, at that moment, she thought of Hudson. She began feeling guilty again.

Greg began moving again. "Is it okay if I cum now?" he asked. His face was strained from holding back.

"Yes," Zoey said. Now she wanted Greg to cum fast as she wanted to get home to be with her boyfriend.

Greg began fucking her harder, and faster. "Is this okay?" he asked. "Can I do this?" he said as he put her legs on her shoulders.

Zoey nodded. She was panting now, gritting her teeth. He was really pounding her now, and she had never gotten fucked so hard by such a big cock. It was a new experience.

As he slammed her pussy, Greg leaned forward so her thighs were pressed against her tits. At that angle, his big cock was rubbing against her clit and g-spot again.

"Oh ... god ...," she softly moaned. It felt really good. And getting pounded like this ... was she going to cum again? So soon? Was it possible?

But a moment later, Greg was cumming. Zoey was glad. She was already feeling guilty enough about Hudson. If Greg made her cum again, she'd feel doubly guilty.

After Greg was done, Zoey quickly got out of bed and hurried to his bathroom with her clothes. She locked the door, then took a quick shower. She spent time washing her face, her breasts and pussy, to remove any trace of Greg. She wanted to be completely fresh when she got home to Hudson.

She quickly dressed. She found Greg waiting outside the bathroom door. "I called an uBer for you," he said.

"Thanks."

"Thanks a lot for tonight. You really took care of my needs," Greg joked with a grin.

"Well, I'm glad," Zoey said with a laugh.

There was an awkward moment of silence. Then Greg leaned in to kiss her.

But Zoey pulled away. "No, we shouldn't," she said. Kissing during sex was one thing. But not after. Or before. Those kind of *romantic* kisses weren't allowed. Those were reserved for her boyfriend. For Hudson.

Greg seemed to get it. They hugged each other, the way platonic friends hug. Then Zoey hurried home to Hudson.

CHAPTER 7

Hudson reclaimed Zoey as soon as she got home. He was extremely aroused, but because he'd already jerked off 3 times that night, he was able to last.

"Your pussy feels so fucking *loose*!" he growled as he fucked her. "Greg really stretched you out! How many times did he use you baby?"

"Twice," Zoey said. "And I went down on him once."

"Oh my god, he really used you!" Hudson moaned. "Did he cum in your mouth?"

"Yes ... and on my face."

"Ohhhhhmyyyyygawwwwd!" Hudson cried as he came.

Afterwards, they were snuggling. "You smell different," Hudson said.

"I took a shower there," Zoey said.

"I guess you smell like his soap," Hudson replied. For some reason, his chest tightened up. He wasn't sure why. Why would it bother him that she smelled like Greg's soap and shampoo? How does that compare at all with sex?

"So ...," Hudson said. "Did it happen? Did you cum?"

Zoey hesitated, then nodded.

Now Hudson's chest really tightened up. The vise around his heart was back. "Wow," he said with amazement. "Wow."

"Hudson, it's no big deal," Zoey said, trying to downplay it.

"Of course it's a big deal," Hudson said back. "I've been trying for years ... and you've had other lovers ... and now Greg gives you the big O on just his third try. What is he, a super stud?"

Hudson was smiling as he said this, but Zoey heard an edge in his voice. She could tell he was hurt and jealous.

"It *really* isn't a big deal," Zoey insisted. "I mean, I'm glad it happened, so I can like, check off that box. But it didn't feel any different."

In truth, it *had* felt different. *Way* different. But if there was ever a good reason for a white lie, this was it.

Then she felt Hudson's cock pressing against her thigh. He was already hard again!

"Wow baby," she said with amazement. Hudson hardly ever got hard again that fast. But lately he had been, when it involved Greg. She was definitely making the connection.

"I guess you need my body again, to take care of your needs," she joked with a grin. Hudson grinned back. Then they were kissing.

After a few moments, Hudson pulled away. They were both panting. He rolled another condom on and got on top of her.

"I'm a little sore," she warned.

"I'll be gentle," Hudson promised, slowly pushing in. "I guess you've been fucked a lot tonight," he teased with a grin. "And Greg really stretched you out. No wonder you're sore."

"You're not mad at me, right?" Zoey asked.

"No, I'm not mad," Hudson assured her. "I love you." Then they kissed as they made love.

CHAPTER 8

Camilla got home from her business trip. Her husband Maynard was waiting for her.

"Drink?" he asked.

"Please."

Maynard mixed Camilla's latest favorite, a Boulevardier. Blanton's bourbon, sweet vermouth, and Campari. The classic recipe was 1-1-1, but Camilla loved bourbon and preferred to soften the bitterness of the Campari, so Maynard had learned to adjust the recipe to 1.25 – 1 – 0.75.

"Thank you," Camilla said as she took a sip. She nodded her head in approval.

"You look lovely tonight," Maynard said as he looked at his wife. "No doubt you were turning heads in first class." Maynard knew his wife always flew first class and stayed in 5-star hotels. She made her company so much money, she could do practically anything she wanted.

Camilla laughed. "Every man there was ancient," she said.

"No doubt they're all in Congress," Maynard joked.

Camilla laughed again.

"I'm sure you found a younger man in Boston to your liking?" Maynard asked.

"I did," Camilla said. "Austin. He turned 18 last Saturday."

"I'm sure the young man enjoyed bedding a hot cougar," Maynard said with a grin.

Camilla smiled back. She didn't sense any insincerity in his voice, or that he was patronizing her. That made her happy. She wanted her husband to know that she still had the face and the body to entice young men into her bed. It was important to her.

"So, is she here?" Camilla asked as she took another sip of the Boulevardier.

"Yes," Maynard said with a nod. "Upstairs."

Camilla willed herself not to shiver.

"You left her alone?" Camilla said as she concentrated to maintain her composure.

"You know I'll always be here to make you your drink," Maynard joked. Camilla laughed.

"So, who is it tonight?" Camilla asked, doing her best to act nonchalant.

"Cagney," Maynard said. "She's in my freshman theater class. Like your Austin, she just turned 18."

Camilla squeezed her eyes shut, forcing herself to keep it together. Maynard smiled. He knew what he was doing to his wife.

"Is she ... is she prettier than me?" Camilla asked.

"Camilla, it's not a fair comparison," Maynard said with a slight smile. "She's 18 and you're 45."

Camilla finally lost it. Her face flushed with excitement, and she moaned.

Maynard's smile grew bigger. He reached out and put this hand over Camilla's breast. Even through her blouse and bra, he could tell her nipple was hard.

"Cagney's breasts are bigger than yours," Maynard said. "And they seem to defy gravity. Her nipples point up towards the ceiling."

"They're better than mine?" Camilla asked, her voice husky.

"You know I love your breasts," Maynard said as he caressed his wife's tits through her clothes. "But breast feeding our two boys, and 45 years of gravity take their toll."

"Oh god Maynard," Camilla moaned, reaching for the countertop as she felt unsteady in her 4-inch Jimmy Choo stiletto heels. "That's not fair. They're your boys."

"You asked if Cagney's breasts are better than yours," Maynard said as he continued to fondle his wife. "I'm just answering your question."

Camilla looked up at her husband. There were tears in her eyes and her face looked tortured.

Maynard took his hand off Camilla and said, "I should get back to Cagney." He poured the rest of the Boulevardier from the shaker into Camilla's martini glass.

"Go ahead," Camilla said. She composed herself, standing up straight in her heels and smoothing her dress. "I'll join you in a moment."

Maynard grinned at Camilla, then moved towards the master bedroom.

They always did it in their master bedroom. Maynard knew that made it even harder for his wife. He enjoyed this. It added delicious spice to his extramarital affairs. Especially since Camilla was so powerful and dominate in every other aspect of their marriage.

After Maynard was gone, Camilla sipped the Boulevardier. She prepared herself for what she was about to see. It was always this way. She had to erect guardrails around her heart. Around her self-respect. Around her dignity. It was never enough though.

She knew once she joined Maynard and Cagney in their bedroom, she would no longer be what they called her at work behind her back – the Dragon Lady. She would be humiliated.

She hated Maynard. Why did he have to have such a pretty face? Such a slim, sexy body? Such a big cock? Yet, she loved Maynard too, and lusted for him, because of all those things.

Camilla's martini glass was half empty when she felt she was ready. She picked up the round bottle of Blanton's and filled her glass to the rim with the sweet bourbon. Her hand was shaking. And her nipples were hard. And her pussy was wet.

Taking a deep breath, she picked up the martini glass and walked in her Jimmy Choos towards the master bedroom.

———— ◆ ————

THE NEXT MORNING AT breakfast, Camilla said, "I have a new assistant. Hudson. He's 26."

Maynard folded the newspaper to look at his wife. He was old school. He enjoyed real newspapers, rather than reading on his iPad.

"Twenty-six?" Maynard said. With a grin, he said, "Isn't that old for you?"

Camilla smiled at the joke. "He's probably not ready for this assignment," she said. "He's arrogant. He doesn't know what he doesn't know."

"Then why pick him?"

"He reminds me of you," Camilla said.

Maynard grinned. "What? A short, skinny pretty boy with a big dick?" He knew his wife's type. His wife's type was *him*.

They both laughed.

"I don't know about the big dick part," Camilla said.

"Are you going to find out?"

"I haven't decided," Camilla answered.

"Then why him?"

Camilla shrugged. She didn't know herself really. "It might be fun," she said. "You know how my job can get monotonous."

"We can't have that," Maynard said.

At that moment, Cagney entered the kitchen. The 18-year-old coed had long, lush dark hair and a beautiful face.

Cagney was naked. Her body was flawless. Large, perfect breasts. Curvy yet firm hips and ass. Flat stomach. Long shapely legs.

Cagney was perfect in every way.

Camilla looked at Cagney as she approached her husband. She hated her.

Cagney took the newspaper from Maynard and tossed it on the floor. She straddled Maynard's legs and wrapped her arms around his neck.

Cagney glanced at Camilla. After last night, she knew Maynard's wife was no threat to her. She was nothing.

She gave Camilla a superior, triumphant look. Then she turned back to Maynard and kissed him. Maynard kissed her back.

Maynard's hands roamed Cagney's perfect 18-year-old body. Cagney reached into Maynard's robe and grabbed his big hard cock. She guided his big manhood into her.

Then Cagney moved up and down on Maynard's shaft, kissing him and caressing his tongue with hers.

Camilla was shaking. From rage, and also from desire. With teary eyes, she reached into her robe and began playing with herself. Her eyes never left the young coed with the beautiful face and flawless body as she rode her husband.

Camilla hated Cagney. And at that moment, she hated Maynard.

And she hated Hudson too. Because she suspected Hudson was just like her husband.

At least Camilla respected her husband. Because, while he was a slim pretty boy, Maynard had a long thick cock. Size mattered a lot to Camilla. It meant power and domination. It was the sign of a real man.

Camilla suspected Hudson was one of those pretty boys with a tiny dick. If he was, then she would have no respect for him. Short, arrogant pretty boys with little dicks didn't deserve her respect.

Camilla refocused her eyes on young perfect Cagney as she fucked the man she loved. Tears fell down her cheeks as she frantically frigged herself.

As Cagney moaned and rolled her head back in orgasm, Camilla came too. Then she dropped to her knees and took hold of her husband's cock, so he could finish in her mouth.

CHAPTER 9

Over the next 6 weeks, Hudson traveled a few days each week with Camilla on business trips. She was a tough boss. They closed a few big deals. Hudson was ecstatic. He felt each deal brought him closer to not only partnership, but a powerful leadership position once he got there. Although, he wasn't sure how he helped close the deals. In fact, it wasn't clear to him what his role was in this joint marketing effort. Still, Camilla seemed pleased with his work – she didn't compliment him, but she didn't criticize either – so he figured he was doing well.

Hudson quickly noted that Camilla was a big time a flirt. She liked male attention.

There was a young waiter. A young businessman. There were many others.

Camilla seemed to like young, men who were Hudson's age, or younger. This typically happened in the bar or at dinner after that day's business meetings.

Hudson wondered if Camilla took these men (boys really) to her hotel room.

Camilla flirted right in front of Hudson. She knew he would keep his mouth shut. It would be professional suicide to blab around the office.

Hudson knew Camilla was married. She wore wedding and engagement rings on her finger, with big sparkling diamonds. Hudson didn't judge Camilla if she was stepping out. After all, he'd cheated on Zoey a few times.

Hudson often caught Camilla looking at him. Not just his face, but his chest, his ass, his crotch. Hudson was used to girls looking at him.

If Camilla wanted to fuck, he would. It wouldn't be a hardship; she was a good looking MILF. And it certainly wouldn't hurt his career. He was an experienced lover. He'd get her off. He also sensed she would keep it to herself, just like he would.

———◦———

USUALLY, HUDSON WAS away for 3 or 4 days a week, and sometimes over weekends. He and Zoey missed each other desperately. It was the most they'd been away from each other since they began dating.

When Hudson was home, they fucked like rabbits. They both liked sex, and even after being together for years, they were still hot for each other.

Hudson rarely saw Greg at work since he was traveling so much, and Zoey had not seen or talked to him since the last time when she had sex with him in his apartment. But they talked about Greg during sex. He was part of their sexy pillow talk.

Hudson wanted to do it again. He told Zoey he wanted to watch him make her cum. He even joked, "Maybe I'll pick up a few tips."

Zoey was skeptical about a repeat. Bringing a third person into a relationship had danger written all over it. Although she did admit to Hudson that she found the "*naughtiness*" of having sex with someone—while at the same time being in a committed relationship—to be a turn on.

Zoey wasn't a prude. She'd done a lot sexually, both before Hudson and with him. For example, she'd lost her anal virginity to him. Hudson also liked to have sex in semi-public places, and she'd gotten into the thrill of that. So, while having a threesome with Greg was outside her comfort zone, she didn't see it as a sin or anything like that. Her concerns mostly stemmed from how it might affect his relationship with Hudson, not that it was sexually deviant.

Zoey admitted that Hudson "ordering" her to let Greg use her body to take care of his sexual needs seriously pushed her sub-space buttons. The couple didn't use whips or chains, but their sexual relationship definitely had a S&M undercurrent to it. Hudson got off on controlling his girlfriend, and she got off on being controlled.

After much cajoling from Hudson, Zoey also admitted that the vaginal orgasm she got with Greg had felt different. She had quickly pointed out though that "it was different, not better. You're the best lover I've ever had baby, and it's not even close." For her, sex was more than physical pleasure, it was also emotions. While she liked Greg as a friend, she loved Hudson.

Zoey told Hudson about how Greg constantly apologized and asked for permission. For her, that was a major turn off (big cock or not). In bed, she wanted to be taken, and that's exactly what Hudson did, and one of the reasons he turned her on so much.

Hudson felt better after Zoey told him this. It made it easier to deal with the jealousy he felt whenever she was with Greg, because he knew Greg was too shy and meek to steal his girlfriend from him. He might have a big dick, but he didn't have the confident and dominant personality that attracted Zoey. Greg wasn't a *Real Man* like Hudson.

Hudson wanted to see Zoey with Greg again. It took him a long time to get his head around the fact that Zoey had cum on Greg's cock during intercourse. The first man to ever make her cum that way. It was a blow to his ego. And frankly, it was humiliating, as it was the first time in his life that he was faced with the limitations of his below average dick. Hudson had a good body, he worked out a lot, but he couldn't do anything about the size of his cock. He had to deal with the reality that he might never be able to give Zoey a vaginal orgasm during intercourse.

Zoey assured him it didn't matter. But to Hudson, it mattered. And it bothered him.

So then, why was he pushing for Zoey to hook up with Greg again? Why did he want to watch the girl he loved cum on another guy's cock?

Hudson didn't know. He couldn't explain it. But he wanted it. He thought about it all the time. He was obsessed by it.

He was horny all the time. More now than ever, and that was saying something.

When he got horny like this, sometimes he needed more than what Zoey could give him. At her core, Zoey was a good girl. And sometimes Hudson needed a bad girl.

He dialed her number on his iPhone. She wasn't in his contacts. He wasn't stupid.

"What are you doing?" Hudson asked when the women answered.

"Watching something stupid on Netflix," Sidney said.

"You want to get together?"

"It's 7, Hudson," Sidney said. "Isn't Zoey waiting for you at home?"

"No problem. I told her I have to work late," Hudson said. "She believed me. I work late a lot."

"Okay. Come over," Sidney said. Without saying anything to each other, they both deleted the call from their phones.

Thirty minutes later, Hudson was in Sidney's bed. They were both naked. They were fucking.

Hudson and Sidney were both beautiful people. Sidney loved looking at Hudson's handsome face and hot bod. He didn't have the biggest dick, but he knew how to use it. Unlike Zoey, Hudson always got Sidney to cum on his cock.

Hudson lusted for Sidney. She was different from Zoey, and he liked different when he cheated. Sidney had dark hair to Zoey's blonde. Her tits were big to Zoey's little high school breasts. Sidney had a curvy, hourglass body to Zoey's petite figure.

There was something else about Sidney that got Hudson off.

Sidney was Zoey's best friend from college.

Zoey introduced Hudson to Sidney soon after they began dating. A few weeks later, they were fucking behind Zoey's back.

Zoey and Sidney were still best friends. Although they didn't see each other often, as their lives were busy. Nowadays, Hudson probably saw Sidney more than Zoey. She didn't know about their hookups, of course.

After they were done, they were both panting and sweating. They were glowing from their orgasms, which had been spectacular. Their sex was always spectacular. They were into each other's looks and bodies. And fucking behind Zoey's back made their sex even more delicious, for both of them.

Hudson didn't linger in Sidney's bed. He quickly showered and dressed. Zoey was trusting but she wasn't an idiot. He needed to get home.

As he was leaving, Hudson cupped and squeezed Sidney's bare breast. Her breasts were big and spectacular. She was much bigger than Zoey.

Sidney smiled and said, "Fucked Zoey's little tits yet?"

Hudson laughed. Sidney always said that. She knew Zoey's little high school breasts weren't big enough to fuck. It was Hudson and Sidney's inside joke.

"You're a bitch," Hudson said, but he said it with a smile. "See you next time."

"Call me soon," Sidney said.

"Like you have a problem getting laid," Hudson joked, looking at Sidney's beautiful face and voluptuous body.

"I can have any man I want," Sidney said. They both knew it was true. She had the man Zoey loved, after all. And he had her BFF.

"I just don't want you to give it all to Zoey. She's pretty and has great legs, but we both know she's flat chested."

Hudson laughed. "Bitch," he said with a grin. Then he was gone.

CHAPTER 10

THE NEXT WEEK....

"HEY BUDDY," HUDSON said cheerfully. "How's it going?"

Greg grinned. "So, you're finally back in the office," he said.

"Just today," Hudson said. "The Dragon Lady's got us traveling first thing next week."

"Well, this might be the last day I see you then," Greg said sadly. "Next Monday's my last day."

Hudson gave him a sympathetic look. "How's the job search going?"

"It's going," Greg said with an upbeat smile. But Hudson could tell the smile was forced. Clearly, Greg hadn't gotten any bites yet on his resume.

"But what are you talking about, the last time I see you?" Hudson said with an encouraging smile. "You and me are buddies. You're not going to disappear on me, or I'll kick your ass."

"Well, I guess that's a compliment," Greg said with a chuckle.

"Of course it's a compliment, you dumb shit," Hudson said with a grin. Then he added, "Besides, Zoey would miss you if she never saw you again."

Greg stared at Hudson for a long moment. Then he asked, "So how is she?"

Hudson grinned and joked, "My traveling's getting to her. She's used to getting laid all the time, and now I'm away 3 or 4 days a week.

I've got fucking blue balls too. And phone sex only goes so far." Then he leaned close and whispered, "You're a stud to her you know."

"I am? Why?" Greg said, his spirits immediately lifted.

"You gave her the big O, buddy boy," Hudson said, grinning and giving Greg a friendly punch in the arm.

Greg looked like he didn't understand.

Hudson whispered "She's never cum from intercourse before. You're the first dude to take her to the promise land."

"Wow, I didn't realize ...," Greg said, shocked.

"It's probably your big dick," Hudson said. "She thinks you hit her g-spot. I guess with most chicks, their g-spot is up front. Even little dicked guys like me can get them off. But Zoey's g-spot is higher up. It takes a big dick like yours to reach it."

"Hudson ...," Greg began, looking worried. "Are you pissed?"

"Do I look like I'm pissed?" Hudson said with a laugh. "I love that girl. I'm happy for her. I want everything for her. And anyway, you're just a big dildo to her. No offense Greg, but you know what I mean. So no, I'm not pissed."

In truth, Hudson was still trying to get his head around this. It hurt his ego, and it made him jealous, that he couldn't get Zoey off with his cock, but Greg could. For some reason though, it turned him on too. It was crazy, he couldn't figure it out. But it was true, his dick got hard whenever he thought about it. Which was a lot.

It helped that Hudson wasn't at all threatened by Greg. Hudson was better looking, had a better body, and was way more successful career-wise. Also, he knew that Greg wasn't Zoey's type. He was too meek, too passive, too accommodating. Zoey was attracted to take charge dudes, arrogant assholes like him.

So, Hudson wasn't worried about Greg stealing his girlfriend from him. Because of that, he was able to indulge in his fantasies without worrying about real life consequences.

"Why don't you come to the loft apartment tonight, for dinner?" Hudson asked.

"I'd like that but, I don't want to impose," Greg said.

"You're not imposing buddy," Hudson said with a grin. "Zoey and I talked about it. She'll be disappointed if you bailed on us."

———◉———

DINNER WAS FUN. ZOEY made scalloped potatoes and tossed a salad, and Hudson grilled steaks. They drank 2 bottles of French red wine as they ate. They talked a little about Greg's job search, but he quickly changed the subject and Hudson and Zoey didn't try to pry.

They talked about sports, gossip about common friends, movies, politics, NYC restaurants and nightlife, everything. Greg was easy to talk to, he was well read, so it was a fun time.

Their dining room table was square shaped and sat 4. Hudson and Greg sat facing each other. Zoey sat between them, but she sat close to her boyfriend.

Zoey and Greg had a few things in common. They both were Democrats (Hudson was a Republican), they liked Broadway musicals, and they liked drama and romantic comedy movies. Hudson was more into sports and adventure movies, although he took Zoey to whatever Broadway shows and movies she wanted to go to.

Hudson opened a 3rd bottle of red wine as they moved to the family room. He suggested they all sit on the long sofa, so they all could see the TV. He turned on a Netflix movie, but no one paid any attention to it. With Zoey sitting between them, the sexual tension in the room began to rise.

Zoey sat close to Hudson with his arm around her. About 15 minutes into the movie (and no one was watching anyway), he said "Greg, how are you at foot massages? Zoey loves them, don't you baby?"

Zoey looked at Hudson for a long moment. Then she looked at Greg and nodded.

Under Hudson's direction, they shifted on the sofa. Zoey shifted sideways so her back was against Hudson's chest, and her feet were in Greg's lap.

Zoey was wearing a blouse and black skirt, and hose. Earlier that evening, she'd taken off her shoes, so she'd been in her stockinged feet all night.

Greg began massaging her feet. As he did, Zoey turned her head so she was looking at Hudson.

Hudson reached to Zoey's front. He began unbuttoning her blouse. Zoey didn't resist. When it was completely unbuttoned, he opened it. He looked at Greg. He was still massaging Zoey's feet, but his eyes were locked on Zoey's lacy bra and sexy flat stomach.

Hudson leaned down and kissed Zoey. As he did, he cupped her bra covered breasts with his hands. He caressed them through the bra.

Greg's hands were now on Zoey's legs. First her ankles, then her calves.

Hudson broke the kiss with his girlfriend. They were both flushed and panting. He moved her so she was sitting up. With the extra space, he pulled the blouse off her shoulders and down her arms. Then he unsnapped her bra and also pulled it off her. Now she was naked from the waist up.

He pulled her back to him. He kissed her again, his hands returning to her now naked tits.

This time Greg didn't need to be told what to do. He reached up and unzipped her short black skirt. Zoey kept kissing Hudson, even as she raised her butt to help Greg pull the skirt down her long shapely legs.

Greg saw she was wearing black thigh highs and black panties. The lace of the stocking tops matched that of the panties.

He saw there was a wet spot in her panties. That meant she was aroused, she wanted this, it wasn't all about doing this for Hudson.

He had gotten her to cum on his cock! He was the first man to ever do that to her! She must want this! Zoey, the girl he'd crushed on since the moment he met her, *she* wanted *him* to fuck her! It was a dream come true! Greg couldn't believe it!

"Take off her panties," Hudson said between kisses.

With shaky hands, Greg pulled the panties down her long sexy legs. He immediately saw they were a thong.

Zoey shuddered and moaned into Hudson's mouth as she felt Greg slide her panties down her stockinged legs. Once again, like the other times with Greg, she felt the wrongness of what they were doing, and it turned her on. The way Hudson and Greg talked about her, talked about her body, talked about what they were going to do to her, it made her feel like an object, a piece of meat, and that turned her on too.

Zoey now was completely naked, except for the thigh high stockings. Hudson pulled her up on the sofa, so again she was sitting up, her back against his front. She was facing Greg, and his eyes were moving up and down her tight, sexy body.

Hudson looked at Greg as he reached to her front and cupped her breasts. "Her tits are perfect, right?" he said. Greg eagerly nodded. "They're small. I call them her little high school breasts. They're small but perfect."

Greg was breathing hard. His cock was so hard it hurt in his pants.

Hudson seemed to realize that. He said to Greg, "Take it out. Let her see it. Take off your clothes."

Greg quickly scrambled out of his clothes. His cock was steel hard. Zoey looked at it. She still couldn't believe something that big thing could fit inside her.

Hudson pressed his lips against her ear and whispered, "That big cock look good to you baby? You gonna cum on that big cock again?"

Zoey swallowed hard and her eyelids fluttered. She didn't say anything though. She was still worried about hurting Hudson's feelings. He assured her he wasn't mad or upset about things, but she still sensed it bothered him that Greg had given her a vaginal orgasm, but he never had.

Hudson returned his attention to Greg. His eyes were hungrily checking out Zoey's naked body, and his hands were still caressing her calves.

"Zoe's got a pretty pussy too, don't you think Greg?" he asked with a grin.

Zoey put her arm over her eyes, like she was hiding. It was humiliating to be talked about in such a blatant way, with her right there. Since she was a submissive bottom, being humiliated turned her on, and Hudson knew that. But still, she couldn't bear to look at Greg as her naked body was exposed to him, and as they talked about her.

"This is pretty too, right?" Hudson said. Zoey felt him reach down her body and put his fingertip on her pubic hair. She kept it neatly trimmed, a small, thin landing strip above her clit. Other than that small patch, her body was completely bare of hair from the neck down, as she got regular waxings (including Brazilians). Hudson paid for everything of course. She could never afford the boutique spas he sent her to on her meager and irregular dancer's income.

"But I've been thinking Zoey should have a high school pussy, just like her high school tits," Hudson said. "What do you think, Greg? Want to help with that?"

Greg stared at Hudson, not understanding.

Zoey's arm still covered her eyes. She heard Hudson opening a drawer – it was the drawer of the coffee table. She heard him take something out. It banged against the drawer, so she knew it was metal. She sensed him reach over and hand whatever it was to Greg.

She felt Greg run his finger over her landing strip. She knew it was him touching her from the angle, and also the hesitate way he touched her. "Are you sure?" he asked Hudson.

Zoey sensed Hudson nod to Greg. "She keeps it to prove to me she's a natural blonde," Hudson said, a grin in his voice.

Then Zoey heard the familiar sound of a person pressing the button of a shave cream bottle. She jerked her arm away, uncovering her eyes. She saw Greg squirting shave cream onto his finger. He also held a razor. He was going to shave off her landing strip!

Hudson held her arms, pinning them down. He said, "Greg, put your elbows on her legs, so she can't move."

"Hudson, Hudson …," Zoey whimpered. They were holding her tight. She couldn't move. The feeling of helplessness, helpless as Greg was about to shave her … not even Hudson, but Greg shaving her … it was so humiliating!

"Oh oh," Zoey whimpered as Greg rubbed the shaving cream over her landing strip.

Then Greg hesitated with the razor. He looked at Zoey. "Are you sure?" he asked her.

"Do not ask her!" Hudson hissed. "It's not her decision! Her body belongs to me! Do as I say!"

"Oh god, Hudson …," Zoey moaned. Her nipples were as hard as diamonds, and her pussy throbbed.

"Do it!" Hudson hissed as he glared at Greg. "Be careful! If you nick her, I will fucking kick your ass!

Then he positioned Zoey so she was looking at Greg. He said, "Watch him as he shaves you. He's gonna turn you into a little teenager. Then we're gonna fuck your little high school pussy."

Zoey whimpered again.

Greg carefully ran the shaver over Zoey's skin. It took only a few swipes. Her landing strip was gone. Now Zoey's body was completely bare of hair except for her head.

Hudson handed Greg a bottle of baby oil. "Rub this over it," he said. Zoey took deep breaths as Greg massaged baby oil over her sensitive skin above her clit, where her landing strip had been just a moment ago.

"Put your finger into her," Hudson ordered. Zoey sucked in her breath as he said this.

Greg pushed his index finger, the one lubricated with baby oil, into her pussy. Zoey moaned as his finger penetrated her.

"She's tight, right?" Hudson asked.

Greg nodded as he huskily said, "Yeah she's tight."

"She's not so tight after you get done with her," Hudson said. He was grinning but there was an edge in his voice. Zoey was looking up at him.

"Finger her Greg. Make her cum," Hudson said. "She'll really be ready to fuck after she cums. The slut always needs it more after cumming."

Greg pushed another finger into her. He fucked her with his index and middle fingers of his left hand, as he rubbed her clit with the thumb of his right hand. Hudson's hands cupped her breasts, rubbing her nipples with his thumbs.

"Ahhh ahhh ahhh ...," Zoey moaned as the two men worked on her body. She was so turned on, it wouldn't be long before she came. "Hudson, kiss me, kiss me," she pleaded desperately. She reached up, wrapping her arms around his neck.

Hudson leaned over and kissed her. They hungrily made out, their tongues dancing. Moments later, he felt his girlfriend cum, her body shuddering, moaning into his mouth.

Hudson abruptly got off the sofa. He shifted Zoey so she was on her hands and knees, in the doggy position. She was still panting, recovering from her orgasm, as Hudson pushed his dick into her pussy. He wasn't wearing a condom. He was inside her bare.

Hudson's eyelids fluttered as he reveled in the intense pleasure of being inside his girlfriend's pussy skin-to-skin. Her sweet pussy was smooth and velvety, and tightly gripped his cock like a closed fist. It was the best pussy he'd ever been inside. Being inside her skin-to-skin was even better, the sensations were exquisite.

Although, for a moment, he naughtily thought about Zoey best friend, Sidney. Her pussy was good too. To be fair, probably as tight as Zoe's. And she usually let him fuck her bareback, because she (unlike Zoey) was on the pill.

Hudson grinned inside. It felt good to be bad.

Hudson fucked Zoey in the doggy position for 15 minutes. He fucked her hard and fast. As always, he hoped she would cum from just intercourse. But she didn't. As he felt his orgasm approaching, he reached under her. He fingered her clit as he continued to pound her from behind. Zoey came moments before he pulled out and came on her back.

Hudson collapsed onto Zoey's back, panting as he came down from his orgasm. He lovingly kissed her shoulder, and the back of her neck.

Hudson collapsed onto the sofa next to Zoey. She was about to move but Hudson ordered, "Don't move. Stay just like that."

Zoey did as Hudson said, remaining in the doggy position with her knees on the edge of the sofa and her arms on the sofa's back.

Hudson used Zoey's discarded blouse to wipe his cum off her back. Then he motioned to Greg. "Go ahead. Your turn. Fuck her," he said.

Zoey had her ass in the air, like she was waiting for Greg to take his turn. Her head rested between her forearms on the back of the sofa, her face buried in her long blonde hair.

Greg quickly got to his feet and moved behind Zoey. His cock was fully hard and pointed like a huge battering ram at her ass. He looked uncertainly at Hudson. "Do I have to use a condom?" he asked. He had seen Hudson enter his girlfriend bare.

"Yes," Hudson said with a nod. "Once a month she's safe. I go bareback. I pull out. But *you* still have to use condoms with her." Hudson rubbed Zoey's toned, flat tummy and said, "If she gets pregnant by mistake, it's going to be my baby. Got it?"

Greg nodded. He was disappointed, but he understood. He rolled a condom onto his cock and pushed into Zoey's pussy. She was still tight, but each time it was getting easier, and it took less time for him to get balls deep inside her.

Greg began moving in and out. He began slow and then got faster, but never as hard and fast as Hudson had been a few moments ago.

When Hudson had talked her into another threesome with Greg, Zoey hadn't thought she would cum from intercourse. Not with her boyfriend there. She'd be too nervous and self-conscious. And part of her didn't want to cum with Greg again.

But as Greg slid in and out of her, it began to feel really good, just like before. In this position, on her hands and knees with Greg behind her, he was stroking her g-spot harder than in missionary, and because of his length, the stroking went on and on.

Also, because of his thickness, his shaft rubbed against her clit too. Not as much as when he was on top, but still some. Enough.

Greg was also kissing her neck just below her ear as he fucked her. And also his hands were underneath, fondling her sensitive, little breasts and gently pinching her nipples. The sensations were amazing. The boy was definitely getting to know her body.

Zoey felt it begin growing inside her. The wave slowly built and got higher and higher. The big wave crested, and seemed to stay there for a long time, suspended high above the ocean. Then finally the wave crashed down. The orgasm hit. It slammed her body.

Zoey screamed when she came, her body shuddering and jerking about uncontrollably. Her fingers clawed at the sofa cushions as her climax roared through her body. When it was finally done, she was left whimpering and feeling rubbery weak like a rag doll.

"Are you okay?" Greg said, tenderly kissing her shoulder and neck. "Was that good?" he said, kissing her shoulder again.

Hudson felt like he was going to lose it. He wanted this, and he got exactly what he asked for – he got to see his girlfriend cum on another man's cock. But he wasn't prepared for the deluge of emotions from seeing it actually happen. He was jealous! And angry!

And now, seeing Greg holding and kissing Zoey in a tender way – in a *loving* way – it made him furious!

"Get the fuck off her!" Hudson screamed at Greg, pushing him away from Zoey. His cock fell out of Zoey and his butt hit the floor.

Hudson pulled Zoey into his arms, kissing and whispering sweet nothings to her. Over her shoulder, he glared at Greg.

After long moments – after Zoey's breathing was normal again, when her head stopped spinning and her body stopped tingling—she gently said, "Hudson baby – Greg hasn't cum yet."

Again, Hudson felt like he was going to lose it! Zoey sticking up for Greg?!

But at his core, Hudson was a fair man. And he was fond of Greg.

"Go ahead and finish him off," Hudson told his girlfriend. Then with a hard voice, he said, "With your hand."

Zoey moved to Greg on the floor. She took off the condom and began stroking his hard cock with her two hands. She needed two hands to do it because his cock was so long, thick and heavy.

Greg's breathing got faster. Zoey's soft delicate hands felt amazing. He softly said to Zoey, "I'm almost there. I'll be done in a minute." Zoey nodded.

Moments later, Greg came. His long legs tensed, and he jerked upwards. Zoey managed to hold on and kept pumping his shaft. Greg's cock exploded with jet after powerful jet of his jism. Most of it splashed against Zoey's chest and fell down her hands.

Seeing Greg's spunk all over his girlfriend inflamed Hudson's desires. He got on the floor and moved between Zoey's legs, in the process pushing Greg away.

Hudson used Zoey's blouse again to wipe Greg's sperm from her chest and hands. Then he was inside her, bareback again, moving in and out.

Hudson was tempted to cum inside Zoe! Get the slut pregnant! That would show Greg who she belonged to!

Hudson said to Greg, "Please leave." It was an order, but not an angry hiss like from moments before. Greg quickly dressed. As he was about to leave, he took a look back.

Hudson and Zoey were kissing and hugging as they made love.

Greg's face fell to his feet. He felt sad and depressed as he left the apartment.

CHAPTER 11

THE NEXT DAY ....

"YOU CAN'T STOP SMILING," Denise said with a grin. She was one of Zoey's dancer friends, and they were both at an audition for an off-Broadway show. "What, you got laid last night? Hudson give it to you good?"

"Ha! You'd like to know," Zoey said with a laugh.

"I *would* like to know," Denise teased with a grin. "I'd love to give your sexy boyfriend a test drive."

"Ha! You wish," Zoey said with a grin back. She was used to her friends saying things like that about Hudson. He was truly a gorgeous man, and very fit. On top of that, he was super smart and had a great job. Everyone thought he was a major catch, and they envied Zoey that he was hers.

Zoey was grinning ear-to-ear, but it wasn't about Hudson though. It was about Greg.

"Oh my god, that boy can fuck," Zoey thought to herself. Her body still tingled from last night. Her pussy was sore, but even that added to the experience, because it was the *reason* it was sore – because Greg had such a freaking huge cock.

Zoey knew Hudson was upset. She loved him, so when he was upset, she was upset. Still, *he* was the one who started this.

Zoey didn't understand it. Hudson hated to see her with Greg, but he loved it too. Even last night, after Greg came all over her, he fucked her again. The entire time (after Greg was gone) he talked about how hot it was to see Greg's big cock stretching her pussy, how her loose pussy got him so hot, and how he loved seeing her cum on that big cock. He said all of this even though she knew he had been upset after seeing Greg made her cum from intercourse. She just didn't understand her boyfriend when it came to all of this.

Still, Zoey couldn't help basking in the post-orgasmic glow from last night. She had seriously never cum so hard. And from a vaginal orgasm! From intercourse! Now she understood what her girls meant when they talked about mind-blowing, life-changing, epic sex!

She didn't tell Hudson any of this, of course.

Just before falling to sleep last night, Hudson had said he wanted to do it again with Greg. Her boyfriend was impossible! And insatiable!

As always, Zoey had misgivings about bringing a third person into their sex life. But for the first time—now that she had experienced Greg's big cock – and cum on that cock for a second time—a part of her hoped it *would* happen again.

⟶⚫⟵

FOR THE FIRST TIME, Hudson felt insecure about his relationship with Zoey. Well, that wasn't quite true. When your girlfriend is a head turner like Zoey, you always had to worry about other men trying to steal her away from you. You always felt a little insecure when dudes literally stopped in their tracks to ogle your girlfriend, and that happened regularly with Zoey.

It was more accurate to say that Hudson had never felt insecure about his *sexual* relationship with Zoey. But now he'd seen her cum on Greg's dick. He heard the sounds she made. He saw the way her body reacted. He saw the looks on her face.

Hudson had never heard Zoey make those sounds with him. He'd never seen her body react that way with him. Never.

Was a big dick really that big a deal? He knew he wasn't the biggest down there, but chicks always told him that size didn't matter. *Zoey* always told him that size didn't matter. But then he saw Greg fuck her last night, and he saw her cum on his cock, and her orgasm hadn't been any normal orgasm. Zoey had actually screamed. She fucking screamed.

Jeez.

And this was with *Greg*. Shy, timid Greg. Nice guy, but not Zoey's type. Hudson wasn't worried about Greg.

But what if a tough guy with a big dick put the moves on Zoey? Might she be tempted? Hudson knew how unique his girlfriend was. Zoey had the face of a movie star and the body of a super model. Her pussy felt a tight velvet glove. She had a sweet bubbly personality. And on top of that, she had a little bad girl in her. The fact she allowed him to share her with another dude – Greg – was all you had to know.

On top of that, Hudson loved Zoey. He knew she was the one. Not to get all romantic mushy about it, but he wanted to grow old with this chick.

So, Hudson did the only thing that made sense. The thing any sane man would do.

He went ring shopping. And later that week, he asked Zoey to marry him. And she said yes. Without any hesitation, Zoey said yes. Hudson put the big perfect diamond on Zoey's finger.

And that was it. It was official now. It didn't matter he didn't have the biggest dick. Or make her cum on his cock.

Zoey officially belonged to him.

CHAPTER 12

Hudson had a lot of time to himself during his business travel. The days were busy, full of back-to-back meetings. He and Camilla always ate dinner together to plan for the next day, but she liked to eat early so they were usually finished by 7pm. Sometimes they might get an after-dinner brandy at the bar – Camilla preferred Pappy's bourbon if they had it—but even then Hudson was typically back in his hotel room by 8pm.

When he was alone in his hotel room, he thought a lot about this *"game"* they were playing with Greg. Zoey was excited about being newly engaged and she spent a lot of her time planning the wedding. She never talked about Greg unless Hudson brought it up, which he supposed was a good thing. He didn't want her fantasizing about another go with Greg.

Or did he?

Part of him wanted her thinking about Greg's big cock. How fucked up was that? What man would want his girlfriend – now his finance – fantasizing about fucking another dude?

Hudson searched the internet to try to figure out these urges inside him. He discovered that a lot of men fantasized about their girls with other men. But his research wasn't very useful, because the guys typically said shit like *"I want this, but I don't know why."* That was *exactly* where Hudson was, so how was that helpful? But even though he wasn't able to answer *why* he had these urges, it was comforting to know other men had the same fantasies.

Alone in his hotel room, Hudson got into the routine of a long, slow jerk off. He could make himself cum fast of course, but instead he edged himself along and indulged his fantasies. He slowly stroked himself, his fist loose to prevent cumming too fast. He found if he used Vaseline, his hand felt like Zoey's sweet pussy when he tightened his fist. He got into the habit of keeping a small plastic jar of Vaseline in his suitcase for his self-gratification.

As he stroked himself, he replayed Zoey's times with Greg in his head. It was weird, but the actual fucking wasn't what turned him on the most. The kissing got him the hottest, and the most bothered. The last time, when Greg had tenderly kissed and consoled Zoey after she came, that was so ... what was the word? How best to describe it?

Delicious.

So incredibly *delicious*.

Seeing Greg kissing Zoey that way, it had gotten him so angry and jealous. It sent him into a rage. But it also got his cock so hard it practically exploded. Hudson was beginning to see the clear link between jealousy and arousal.

As he stroked himself, Hudson did more than replay Zoey's times with Greg. He also played out scenarios in his head.

When he did this, he always went back to the evening Zoey had been alone with Greg in his apartment. She'd gone there (at his urging) to console Greg after Camilla had told him he wasn't making partner and would have to find a new job.

That evening had been devastating for Hudson. It was like Zoey had been on a date with Greg. Like, she was *Greg's* girlfriend instead of his. And he was alone by himself in the loft apartment, waiting for Zoey to return home to him.

Hudson always stroked himself harder when he thought about that night. The evening had been dreadful, but so arousing. Sometimes he imagined Zoey going over to Greg's when he was on these business trips. They were friends after all, it was socially acceptable for her to hang out with Greg even though she was engaged to be married.

Especially if her fiancée – Hudson – gave her his permission.

Especially if everyone knew the guy she was hanging with – Greg – was a loser who had no chance with Zoey.

Of course, those people didn't know about Greg's big dick. And how Zoey screamed – *screamed!* – when Greg fucked her with that big dick.

What would Greg and Zoey do together? Spend a long time making out? Touching? Greg making Zoey cum on his big cock? And then tenderly kissing her as she came down from her orgasm?

Hudson played this scene in his head, his lubricated fist closing tighter around his hard cock. He came hard, his body shuddering and his soulful moan like a shout in his darkened hotel room. His intense orgasm left him panting. Afterwards, he felt sick at the idea, like he wanted to throw up. But the next night, he'd be in a different hotel room, and he'd play this scene again in his head as he jerked off with his Vaseline slicked hand.

———◦———

IT WAS A BLOW TO HUDSON'S ego that he couldn't make Zoey cum from intercourse. It was worse since Greg could.

Sometimes he got mad at her. It was her fault, not his. He'd been with lots of girls, including her best friend Sidney, and none of those girls ever complained. They fucking came on his cock.

And don't even try to say they faked it. Hudson wasn't stupid. He could tell.

Sometimes in the evening, after dinner with Camilla, Hudson went to a bar. He'd order a Highland Park and then wait. Watch whatever game was playing on the TV, or surf on his phone. Whatever. He'd wait. And he never had to wait for long.

Hot chicks were everywhere. They were always checking him out. People said he looked like a model, or movie star. And Hudson dressed like a power broker in expensive suits. He *was* a power broker. He was a *Master of the Universe*. Hot chicks could tell. He was more than just his handsome face and beach bod, he was a young man with a very high ceiling. These girls wanted him.

So, Hudson would cruise into a happening bar, and eventually a girl would sit next to him and strike up a conversation. Flirt with him. She was trying to pick him up. Maybe she was looking for a husband, or maybe just a good time.

Hudson was always polite. He was a chivalrous guy. He was always nice to girls. Even the dogs. In fact, he was nicer to the dogs. It wasn't the chick's fault she was ugly.

Like everyone, he had a type he preferred. For Hudson, it was blonde ... sweet face ... little tits ... leggy ... short skirt ... high heels. Just like Zoey.

But at these times, he wanted the opposite. Brunette ... mysterious face ... big tits. He still wanted long legs, short skirts and high heels. Somethings never changed.

Hudson wasn't hung up about age. He preferred young 20-somethings, but he wasn't opposed to older. 30s, 40s, he was okay with that. Even early 50s, if she had a pretty face and a tight body. He liked younger too, of course. But legal. He wasn't a pervert.

If the girl checked off all his boxes, Hudson might flirt back. Buy her drink. Maybe caress her knee as they laughed and talked. Brush his hand across the side of her big bust.

And yeah, sometimes he'd take the girl up to his hotel room. Not often, but sometimes. Hudson was a man. A *Master of the Universe*. He was entitled.

And he was careful. Zoey would never find out.

With Zoey hooking up with Greg, he found he needed an ego boost.

And with Zoey cumming on Greg's big cock – and especially with Greg's cock being so much bigger than his – he needed an ego boost even more.

Tonight, he was in Chicago, and after giving Zoey a good night phone call, Hudson splashed on some cologne and headed to a whiskey bar he'd read about, *Baptiste*. The review said "This is the bar where the beautiful people go. The men are handsome and fit, and the girls gorgeous with very long legs. And the whiskey is good too."

As Hudson walked through the crowded bar, he sensed girls checking him out. He pretended not to notice.

Hudson knew this was the place to be when he saw their drink menu had 5 pages of scotch. He ordered a Highland Park Single Cast 30 year. He had read about this scotch but this was the first time he had ever seen it offered. It was $150 for a 2 oz pour. He didn't care how much it cost. He deserved it. He was a *Master of the Universe.*

A few minutes later, a woman slid into the seat next to him. She crossed her legs as she sat down. "Is this taken?" she asked Hudson. "Are you waiting for your wife?"

Hudson shook his head. "I'm here on business," he said.

"Same," the woman said. She was looking at Hudson, checking him out.

Hudson decided to do the same to her. She was fortyish. Brunette with soft curls and reddish highlights. Pretty face. Brownish red lipstick. Big tits in an expensive dress. Long legs. Hose. Expensive high heels. Wedding ring.

She checked all the boxes. They began to talk. Laugh. Flirt. Her name was Dana. She was from Boston.

Dana was drinking a Manhattan, up, with a Maraschino cherry. She asked Hudson what he was drinking and he told her. She was interested. She said she loved bourbon, but with a pretty smile said, "when I grow up I want to drink scotch." Hudson grinned at her. It was a cute thing to say.

Hudson offered her a taste. Dana took a sip. She left lipstick on his tumbler. It looked fucking sexy. It caused him to look at her lips. Dana caught him looking.

Most men would quickly look away, pretending like he hadn't been staring. That wasn't Hudson. Instead, he confidently joked, "I'm the kind of creep who looks at a girl's lips when she talks." Dana laughed. Hudson could tell she liked him.

When their glasses were empty, he offered to buy them both a round of Highland Park Single Cast 30 year. She said it was too expensive. She touched Hudson's hand with hers, and suggested he buy just one, and they share it.

"I don't have cooties, I promise," Dana joked. They both laughed.

Dana reapplied her lipstick just as the waiter arrived with a fresh glass filled with two ounces of the expensive scotch. Her lips looked wet from the lipstick. It looked fucking sexy. For a moment, Hudson imagined those lips around his cock. She smiled as he looked at her, thinking the same thing.

They passed the glass back and forth, taking sips as they flirted. Each time the glass was passed, their fingers would touch. And each time Dana took a sip, Hudson's eyes lingered on her brownish red lipstick on the rim of the tumbler. The sexual tension between them continued to grow.

Somehow, they got onto the topic of bare leg versus wearing hose. Dana said she always wore hose, because it was too cold in Boston to go bare leg, and Chicago was just as cold. Hudson said, "Thank god for snow." Dana laughed at his stupid joke like it was the funniest thing she ever heard.

Dana crossed and re-crossed her legs. Each time, her skirt hiked up, showing more firm thigh. Hudson looked, and he didn't try to hide it.

"You're supposed to at least pretend you're not checking me out," Dana said with a grin.

"Why would I do that?" Hudson said, grinning back. Dana laughed.

Hudson daringly put his hand on Dana's knee. She didn't push his hand away. They both were looking at his hand on her knee when he began caressing her with the pad of his thumb.

Dana said, "You're too good looking to be single. Married?"

Hudson said, "I'm engaged."

"What's her name?"

"Zoey," Hudson said, saying his fiancée's name as he continued to caress another woman's knee.

"Zoey's a lucky girl," Dana said, her cheeks becoming flushed from Hudson's caresses. She looked at his hand on her leg and said, "Your touch is nice. I hope Zoey appreciates it."

"She does," Hudson said. "But I've been traveling a lot lately."

"So that's why you're here talking to a strange woman?" Dana teased.

As she said this, she moved her leg slightly, so the pointy toe of her high heel pressed against Hudson's ankle. He sucked in his breath at the sexy feel of the hard leather pressing into his skin.

Hudson shrugged, not answering her question. Instead, he said, "You're married." He was looking at Dana's wedding ring on her left hand.

"I am," she confirmed. She pressed the toe of her high heel harder into Hudson's ankle, making him breath even harder.

For some reason, Hudson found the fact that Dana was married to be incredibly arousing. It was like the reverse of Greg fucking his girl. *Now* Hudson was with another man's girl. It was evil, and strangely arousing.

"How long have you been engaged?" Dana asked.

Hudson moved his hand higher up Dana's leg, onto her inner thigh, and she gulped. "How long have you been married?" he asked.

"Okay, so don't answer my question," Dana said with a laugh. "Kyle and I have been married for 15 years. I got married when I was 27." After a moment, she grinned and said "Yes, that means I'm 42."

Hudson was 26. She was 16 when he was born. For some reason, he found that thought intensely arousing.

Still stroking her inner thigh, he said "You're a very hot MILF."

Dana giggled like a schoolgirl, clearly happy with his complement. "I'm not a MILF," she said. "I don't have any children. It was by choice. I wanted to keep my body."

Hudson looked at Dana, intrigued by her words. She kept her body hot to, what? To keep her husband Kyle happy? Or to be able to pick up handsome young men in bars? Hudson found that idea to be incredibly arousing. He was hard in his pants.

"Maybe I won't let Zoey get pregnant," he said. "So she keeps her tight body."

Dana laughed. She wasn't offended by what Hudson said.

Hudson moved his hand from Dana's leg to a pendant around her neck. "A gift from Kyle?" he asked.

Dana nodded. "Our last anniversary," she said.

Dana's dress formed a V, providing a hint of her substantial cleavage. Hudson slid his fingertips down Dana's chest, along the center of the V. She was breathing hard. Hudson could feel her heart pounding.

"This is very nice," Hudson said, tracing the soft swell of her cleavage with his fingertip.

"You're very sure of yourself, aren't you Hudson?" Dana asked, reflecting on how he was opening touching a woman he barely knew in the middle of a bar. And a married woman at that. "You're a very confident man.

It was the way she said, "*confident man.*" It gave him a brief window into her soul. With a taunting voice, he said, "Is that why you're here Dana? Your husband's not man enough for you?"

Hudson half expected Dana to slap his face at saying something so demeaning about her husband. Instead, the 42-year-old cougar softly moaned.

Hudson trailed his hand down her front. His fingertips drifted over her nipple – he felt it was hard, even though her dress and bra – and moved back down to her leg. He inched his fingers under the skirt of her dress.

"Uncross your legs Dana," Hudson ordered. She hesitated, then uncrossed her legs, although she kept her knees pressed together.

Hudson's hand continued its journey up her skirt. He touched lacy stocking tops. "Very sexy Dana," he said approvingly.

Then his hand moved farther. He touched her bare skin above her stockings. Soft firm skin. Dana shuddered at the feel of his fingers on her bare skin.

Then his fingertips were at her panties. She was soaking wet. He felt prideful knowing he had gotten her that way. She softly moaned as he pressed his fingertip over her panty-clad clit.

"I'm staying at this hotel," Dana whispered in a lustful, throaty voice.

"What room?" he asked.

"329," Dana said without hesitation.

Hudson nodded. "I'll meet you there."

Hudson was careful. He never wanted Zoey to find out.

Dana stood up as Hudson called the bartender over for another drink.

"Hurry," Dana urgently whispered.

Hudson took his time, sipping the scotch for 15 minutes. Finally, he paid the check and head over to room 329.

He felt like a *Man*. He was going to fuck a sexy cougar. Get her to cheat on her husband. Fuck her better than her husband.

Hudson knew Greg would have no chance with a girl like Dana. No chance. She wouldn't give him the time of day. She'd laugh in his face if he made a move on her.

But Dana had come onto *him*. She saw how handsome he was. She saw his hot body. Dana picked *him*! She wanted *him*!

So, fuck Greg. And frankly, fuck Zoey. He was a *Master of the Universe*. He could get all the pussy he wanted.

CHAPTER 13

Zoey was busier than ever. She had auditions a few times a week, and her agent felt she was close to landing a gig. She worked out regularly, to stay hot for Hudson and keep her dancer's body. And now, on top of all that, she had a wedding and honeymoon to plan.

Often during the day, she looked at her new engagement ring and felt giddy, her knees going weak. The diamond was huge! And the platinum setting was so elegant and beautiful!

She loved it!

She was so excited to be Hudson's fiancée. She loved him so much. They were getting married! She felt like she was in a dream.

And sometimes, she thought about Greg. She couldn't help it. Especially with Hudson traveling so much. She was lonely. And horny!

And the sex with Greg ... *god* ....

Was it more possible to underestimate someone? It was like, you see a man jogging on the street, and you say, okay that's a normal person, just an ordinary person going for a run, and then he breaks the freaking marathon record.

That was Greg. He was a normal guy. Shy. Scared of his own shadow. Kind of cute in that *Bill Nye the Science Guy* way.

But then you find out he has this big dick. And he can fuck like nobody's business.

God ....

He made her cum so hard. From intercourse! It was so intense she practically blacked out.

For the first time in her life, she really understood what a *"toe curling"* orgasm was.

She actually had a hard time sitting on their sofa. It made her think *"That's where Greg fucked me from behind, and made me cum on his freaking huge cock!"*

Tonight, when Hudson called, they had phone sex. He said he wanted to see her with Greg again. He said he wanted to see her cum on his big cock again.

Hudson said they were young. They were in love and engaged to be married. Why not sow some wild oats before the wedding? Greg was safe. They trusted him, he would never tell anyone. Zoey clearly got off on it. So did Greg. So did Hudson. So why not? It was a win-win-win.

Zoey still had misgivings about bringing a third person into their sex life. It wasn't right, that she'd be browsing a catalog for a wedding dress, and then her thoughts would drift to Greg fucking her. She'd get wet, her pussy would begin throbbing, and then she'd have to freaking beat off. It wasn't freaking right!

But if Hudson wanted her to do it ...

He was her man. She was his girl. She wore his ring. She belonged to him.

If Hudson wanted her to do it ... well, it was easier for her to do it then.

Zoey looked at their sofa again. In fact, Greg had taken her there 3 times. And once on his bed. Four times. If Hudson had his way, would she get to the point where she lost count?

⎯⎯⎯◈⎯⎯⎯

HUDSON CALLED GREG the next morning. The morning after he cheated with Dana.

Dana said he fucked her better than her husband. As they fucked, he got Dana to say her husband was a loser. Hudson got off on that.

They were both too smart to exchange numbers. That was how you got caught. One-night stands were best. And it wasn't like Hudson couldn't get more pussy, or the hot cougar Dana couldn't get more dick. So why take the chance?

Anyway, Hudson called Greg. He was feeling better about himself after fucking Dana. Who cared if he couldn't get Zoey off on his cock? He *certainly* got Dana off on his cock.

Hudson and Greg chatted and caught up. Greg told Hudson he was thinking about opening his own business, as a financial planner. Hudson told Greg he was still traveling 3 or 4 days a week.

After their chit chat, Hudson said, "I want you to get a sex test. For STDs."

Greg hesitated, then said "Okay. Does that mean—."

"I haven't decided," Hudson told him. "But it's possible."

"Okay, then I'll get tested," Greg said.

"I'll need to see the results," Hudson said.

"Sure, of course," Greg said.

"You understand what this means, right Greg?" Hudson said. "You can't be with any other girls."

"Well, I told you how pathetic I am at meeting girls," Greg said with a sheepish chuckle.

"I'm serious Greg," Hudson said sternly. "If we're doing this, that means you don't put your dick in other girls. It'll be up to Zoey to take care of your needs. Just her."

"I'm okay with that," Greg hesitantly said.

"And I'm not promising how often it'll happen," Hudson warned. "So, you'll have to live with blue balls."

"I'm okay with that," Greg said again.

"Okay then," Hudson said.

He grinned inside, and thought, "I *am* a Master of the Universe. Not only do I control Zoey's body, I control Greg's too. I control when they both get laid. I can deny them both if I want. I can order them to give each other ruin orgasms. That would be fun. All the while I can fuck sexy things like Dana and Sidney all I want. I'm like Thanos. I am inevitable."

Hudson laughed to himself about Thanos. He loved those movies.

"Hudson, are you there?" Greg asked.

"Yeah," Hudson said, pulling himself out of his reverie. "So, what are you doing today?"

"Nothing."

Hudson nodded. "Stay close to your phone," he told Greg. "Zoey might be calling you."

⸺●⸺

"I WANT YOU TO CALL Greg," Hudson said over the phone to Zoey a few minutes later.

"Hudson ... seriously?" Zoey said incredulously. She was still getting her head around this. Hudson, the man she loved, the man she was going to marry, he was sharing her with another man.

"You're not even here," she said.

"I'll be home tomorrow night," he reminded her. "I'll be able to think about you all day. I'll get off on it."

"You want me to call him now?" Zoey said, still incredulous. "I just ate breakfast."

"Sure. Why not? He's not working. You don't have an audition today."

"I was going to work out today."

"So, take Greg with you," Hudson said. "He's probably been sitting around all day and eating Oreos. He's getting flabby probably. He was never that ripped anyway. He could probably use a workout."

It made Hudson feel good to put Greg down. It was like he was saying to Zoey, *I'm better than Greg in every way. Yeah, he's got a bigger cock, but he's just a human dildo.*

Zoey was silent, not responding to Hudson's dig of Greg.

After a moment, Hudson said, "Greg agreed not to hook up with other girls."

"What?" Zoey said, shocked.

"He's swearing off other girls," Hudson said. With a chuckle he added, "You've got his big dick all to yourself."

"Hudson, seriously?" Zoey said in disbelief. "Why would he do that?"

"It's not like he's scoring with other girls," Hudson said.

"Hudson, will you be nice," she said with a frown in a voice.

"I'm not being a jerk," Hudson insisted. "Greg said that himself."

"I know but ... why would he agree not to be with other girls? Does he think I'm always going to be there for him?"

"No, I told him there were no guarantees," Hudson assured her. "It's completely up to you."

"Well thanks for that," Zoey said with a sarcastic laugh.

"I'm not kidding Zoe honey," Hudson said into the phone. "Yeah, we play dom and sub games. But I'm not *really* a Neanderthal. I know it's your body. It's up to you what you do with Greg. I'm just saying, we all get off on it, so it's a win-win-win."

"But you still haven't said why he'd agree to not have sex with other girls," Zoey pressed.

"I told him I might let him do you without a condom," Hudson said. "I told him to get tested. Obviously, that means he can't be with other girls after he gets tested."

"He can just get tested again," Zoey pointed out.

"Well, I guess," Hudson said. With a laugh, he said, "I guess I like the idea of Greg with blue balls when he's not getting it from you. You know. Denying him sex."

"Hudson, this is freaking crazy," Zoey lamented. "I know you said this is the time for us to sow wild oats, but this is freaking crazy."

"I just need to control things," Hudson said, opening up to his fiancée. "Greg is getting to fuck his wet dream. You're getting off on his big cock. I'm up for all of that. But I need to control things. You're my girl. Greg might be getting some of you, but you're *my* girl. Do you understand what I'm saying?"

Zoey heard vulnerability and anxiety in Hudson's voice. He rarely opened up to her like this. It melted her heart. "Hudson baby, we don't have to do this," she said with a tender, loving voice. "You're all I want. And need."

"I want to do this," Hudson insisted. "I'm fucking getting off on it."

"But without a condom?" Zoey asked doubtfully.

"I haven't decided babe," Hudson said excitedly. "But it gets me hot, thinking about Greg filling your pussy with his cream."

Zoey could tell he was really excited. She asked, "Are you playing with yourself baby?"

"Oh yeah babe," Hudson said. "I'm using Vaseline. My hand feels like your sweet pussy."

"Oh god Hudson," Zoey giggled. "It feels good?"

"Not as good as your pussy, but it'll do until I get home," Hudson said. Zoey giggled again.

"Are you wet baby?" he asked. "Have you been thinking about another go with Greg?"

"I ...," Zoey hesitantly said, her voice trailing away. Then she decided to come clean. "Yes, I've thought about it."

Hudson felt his insides seizing up, that big vise twisting his guts again. Zoey was thinking about Greg! Thinking about his big dick!

"Oh god Zoe baby," he moaned. "That's so fucking hot! You're thinking about riding Greg's big cock again! That's so hot babe! God I love you so much!

Zoey was breathing hard now. Her pussy was beginning to throb. "That really gets you hot baby?" she asked.

"Yesssss!" Hudson lustfully hissed.

"I can't look at our freaking sofa without thinking about Greg fucking me from behind," she told him.

"Oh god! Fuck! You're gonna make me fucking cum!"

Zoey ran her hand over the flat of her stomach and reached into her tights. She shivered as she touched her clit. "Is Greg really giving up other girls for me?" she asked Hudson as she fingered herself.

"Oh yeah, he is," Hudson said excitedly. "You're it babe. He's got only you to take care of his needs."

"God baby ...," Zoey moaned. "And that's what you want? You want me to let Greg use my body for his needs?"

"Yesssss!" Hudson hissed. "And I want you to do it today. I want to think about Greg fucking you, and you cumming on his big cock. I want to think about you screaming like last time, screaming as he makes you cum."

———◆———

AFTER HANGING UP WITH Hudson – after they both came – it took Zoey some time to compose herself. And to think about what to say. How exactly does a girl ask a boy if he wants to hook up? This was new territory for her, since every other time in her life, it was the man who instigated things.

It made it easier that she'd already been intimate with Greg. But it was still freaking crazy, since she was – *hello!* – engaged to be married with a big rock on her left hand.

But she had to admit ...

She had to admit ...

She wanted to feel Greg's big cock in her again.

Zoey called Greg. "So hey," she began.

"Hi," Greg said.

"It's me. Zoey."

"Yeah I know," Greg said with a smile in his voice. "I know your voice. And your name comes up on my phone."

"Yeah, okay, right," Zoey said with a laugh. She felt stupid. "This is still kinda awkward."

"Yeah, I know."

"Did you really say that to Hudson?" Zoey asked. "About other girls?"

"Yeah, I mean, you're worth it," Greg gushed.

Zoey was rendered speechless by his words. It wasn't what he said. That could be just a line to get into her pants. It was how he said it. He was so sincere, so genuine. Greg was transparent. He wore his heart on his sleeve. Zoey knew it wasn't a line. It was the truth.

She found it incredibly charming, and endearing.

"So anyways," she sputtered. "Are you doing anything? Do you want to hang out?"

"Sure," Greg said immediately. "Do want me to come over to your place?"

Zoey thought about it. She looked at the sofa. They could do it there again. But if she was going to do this, she wanted to be on a bed. It couldn't be her bedroom. Not the bed she shared with Hudson. That seemed over the line, like kissing Greg outside of sex. They had a guest room, but all they had was a single bed, they'd probably end up falling off as Greg was a tall boy.

Greg had a bed though. It wasn't as nice as the bed she shared with Hudson. But it would do.

"I'll come over to you," she told him.

———◆———

NOW ZOEY HAD TO DECIDE what to wear. She dressed to impress for Hudson. To make his dick hard. She didn't do that for Greg or any other man.

Zoey took a shower. She put her hair up in a ponytail. No makeup.

She picked out skinny jeans and a long sleeve stretchy top. Black ankle boots with a little heel. It was the kind of thing she'd wear around their apartment. She did pick out a sexy bra and matching thong panties. And she put on pantyhose too, under the skinny jeans.

She felt comfortable in pantyhose. As a dancer, she'd worn tights most of her life. She also knew that men found pantyhose under jeans to be sexy. Hudson certainly did. And she already pegged Greg as a leg man, just like her fiancée.

Thirty minutes later she was in Greg's apartment. This time she noticed the bookstore – Java Books—as she walked up the one flight to where he lived. She also smelled the rich expresso aroma of their coffee machines.

"Hey," Zoey said when Greg let her in.

"Hey," Greg said back. He hungrily looked her up and down, eating her up with his eyes. He moved forward to take her into his arms, but Zoey stepped back.

"Can we, like, do something?" Zoey asked. "You know, hang for a little bit?"

Zoey didn't want to go straight to sex. That would feel too much like a booty call, a one-night stand, and that wasn't Zoey. She needed to have some connection with a man to have sex with him. Yes, they'd already done it before. But those times, Hudson had been there. Even the time she winded up alone in Greg's apartment, she'd been with Hudson before. Now though he was away on a business trip. Zoey would feel like a cheap slut if she immediately jumped into bed with Greg.

"Sure, how about getting coffee downstairs?" Greg suggested. Zoey nodded. That was a good idea.

———— ◉ ————

JAVA BOOKS SMELLED like old books and coffee. Which, surprising, wasn't a bad combination. It was nice, comforting.

To get to the coffee part of the store, you had to pass through tall shelves all packed with used books for sale. Signs said "$1.50 for paperbacks" and "$5 for hardbacks." There was an alcove full of old magazines. Another alcove was full of old vinyl records. Jazz music was softly playing in the background.

An old man was behind the counter in the little coffee bistro at the back of the store. He had to be at least 70. Greg introduced him as Jacob. He owned Java Books.

It was clear Jacob and Greg were friends. They chatted as he made their expresso drinks. Greg ordered a cappuccino. Zoey ordered a skinny vanilla latte with non-fat whip.

Jacob had his eye on Zoey as he chatted with Greg. He was surprised his young friend was with such a pretty girl. Then he noticed the ring on Zoey's finger. He frowned but didn't say anything.

Zoey and Greg sat in a corner table. They sipped their coffees as they chatted and caught up. She asked about his job search. Greg said he was thinking about going out on his own as a financial planner. Zoey told Greg she was closed to landing a gig. It was off Broadway, but it was a musical and she'd get to dance, and it was even a speaking part.

Greg was excited for her. He promised to be there opening night. He'd seen her dance before, and he thought she was amazing.

Zoey looked down at her feet, and even blushed, as Greg heaped this praise on her. If it was any other guy, she'd think it was a line to get into her pants. But Greg was so sincere and genuine. She could tell by his voice. He really meant what he said. So, his compliments made her feel warm inside.

Greg asked Zoey what she liked to read. Zoey admitted she didn't read books much. She mentioned, though, that she was thinking about reading *Emma*. She'd watched the movie a few weeks ago on Netflix with Hudson and loved it.

Greg immediately jumped up. "I'll be right back," he said as he hurried off. A few minutes later, he returned with a hardbound book. "*Emma*" by Jane Austen.

"Oh," Zoey said surprised. "Thanks but ... I was going to get it for my Kindle."

Greg shook his head. "It's so much better to read real books," he said enthusiastically. "Holding a book in your hand, especially a hardback book, it makes the experience so much better."

Greg bought the book for Zoey as a gift. It would be the first of many gifts he would give her.

Zoey and Greg read their books as they sipped their coffee. She hadn't noticed but he had brought a book with him. She would learn that he almost always had a book with him, if only a paperback in his back pocket. Greg was usually reading 4 or 5 books at the same time, switching between them depending on his mood.

It was quiet time, both of them reading, not saying anything. Zoey reflected that it was so different with Hudson. Life with Hudson was non-stop action, always doing something. It was an exciting life, but hardly ever did they just sit for a quiet moment. The closest they came was in the morning when Hudson read all the financial news on his iPad as he drank coffee. Even then though, he usually had ESPN or a financial news show playing in the background.

Zoey realized it was nice sitting here with Greg, reading and sipping coffee. It was comfortable. It felt familiar being with him.

They were sitting close because the round table was small. Their knees were almost touching. Zoey finished a chapter and took a moment to look at Greg. He was a big man, tall and lanky. He was cute. Not gorgeous like Hudson. But definitely cute. And taller than both Zoey and Hudson. If he did something with his hair, he might even be handsome. He might even be hot.

The mornings were busy at Java Books, and Jacob was busy making expresso drinks for his customers. He kept his eye on his young friend Greg though, and the pretty girl he was sitting with at the two top in the back. The two of them were sitting close, closer than casual platonic friends would be sitting.

Greg had introduced her as Zoey. She was wearing an engagement ring. Greg said she was engaged to Hudson, his friend from work.

But Jacob had seen Zoey before. She was so pretty, you wouldn't forget seeing her. Jacob had seen Zoey leaving Greg's apartment a few weeks ago. And the walls and ceilings in his old building were thin, especially in his office which was directly below Greg's apartment. Just before seeing Zoey leave, Jacob had heard the sounds of Greg having sex with a girl in his apartment. It must have been Zoey. And when he saw Zoey leave that evening, Jacob was pretty sure she wasn't wearing an engagement ring.

Greg got up and told Zoey he wanted to grab a couple books for later. He was looking in the stacks when a girl approached him. They began talking.

The girl was wearing a name tag so she worked at Java Books. Zoey was too far away to read the girl's name.

The girl had short brown hair in a pixie haircut. She was cute in a homespun kind of way, like Emma Watson (although this girl was Asian). She was about Zoey's height and petite (again like Zoey). Zoey had small breasts, but no one would call her flat chested (unless they were joking with her, as Hudson often did). But this girl *was* flat chested.

Zoey watched Greg talk to the girl. They clearly knew each other. Were they flirting? Zoey frowned, feeling jealous that Greg was flirting with another girl. Touching her engagement ring on her finger, she knew that made no sense, but she couldn't help how she felt.

Greg and the girl walked over. "Hey Zoey," Greg said. "This is my friend Kimmy."

"Hi," Zoey said with a friendly smile.

"Hi," Kimmy said back. She gave Zoey a quick up and down look. She tightened her jaw at seeing how pretty Zoey was. Not just pretty, but gorgeous. And who had such long legs? This girl was a 10, and Kimmy knew ... well, she knew she was cute, but not a 10. Then she noticed Zoey's engagement ring. She looked relieved. *"She's engaged,"* Kimmy thought to herself. *"Greg and Zoey are just friends."*

Jacob called Kimmy over. She said quick goodbyes, then joined Jacob behind the counter.

Zoey eyed Kimmy making a panini, then grinned at Greg. She whispered conspiratorially, "So who is she? You look like you're friends."

"We *are* friends," Greg said.

"I mean friends friends," Zoey said with a grin. "She's clearly into you."

"Well, we've dated a few times," Greg admitted with a sheepish smile.

"Okay ...," Zoey said expectantly. She impatiently waved her hands as she said "Details?"

"That's it. We dated a few times," Greg said with a shrug.

"Have you had sex?" Zoey asked.

"I mean, that's kind of private," Greg sputtered.

"Seriously Greg?" Zoey asked, giving him a *what-the-fuck* look. Translation: After all we've done, you can't tell me if you've fucked that pretty Asian girl?

"Okay, we've messed around a little," Greg admitted. Then he whispered, "But Kimmy's a virgin. She wants to wait until she's married."

Zoey sat back, her mouth opening in surprise. "Oh. Wow."

"I mean, she's only 19, she's still in college," Greg said. "She's kinda too young for me anyways."

"Yeah, I guess ...," Zoey said. She shook her head at Greg's bad luck. He talked about having problems finding girls. Then he finds a girl who's into him, but he can't have sex with her because she's a virgin and wants to wait until she's married.

At that moment, Zoey got a text from Hudson. It said, "Are you with Greg?"

Zoey: "Yes. We're in the bookstore in his building."

Hudson: "Send me a picture. Make sure it shows all of you. I want to see what you're wearing."

Zoey couldn't help grinning. Hudson was such a bad boy. She loved it.

Zoey got Jacob to take a picture of her and Greg. She texted the picture to Hudson. Then she and Greg went up to his apartment.

⸺⬥⸺

HUDSON STARED AT THE picture. Zoey and Greg were standing next to each. Close, almost touching. They were both smiling into the camera.

Zoey was casual, her hair in a ponytail and no makeup. Jeans and one of those stretching tops she always wore at home when they were relaxing. She looked beautiful and sexy, but she hadn't dressed up for Greg. That made Hudson feel better.

Hudson looked at her feet. She wore ankle boots, not high heels. If she was with him, even dressing casually, she would have worn spiky high heels. But since she was with Greg, she didn't. That made him feel better too.

Hudson zoomed in on the picture. Zoey's skinny jeans were capri-type. They ended above her ankles. Above the ankle boots. With the zoom, he saw that Zoey was wearing pantyhose under her jeans.

The vise gripped Hudson's heart. Butterflies bolted through his stomach. Zoey put on pantyhose under her jeans! For Greg! She dressed up for Greg!

And now they were having coffee together! They were on a date!

Jealousy roared inside him. It gripped his gut, twisted it around. But yet, he was so aroused. It was so fucking delicious. His cock was steel in his pants.

He had to stop thinking about this. He had meetings all day with Camilla. He couldn't be distracted. He couldn't fuck up.

He still wasn't sure if he was doing a good job at the meetings. Camilla seemed to be handling the meetings by herself. He barely said anything. Why did she even need him?

Hudson texted Zoey: "Remember to stream to that site."

Hudson had set it up in advance. Zoey would video her sex with Greg and stream it to a secure site. Only Hudson and Zoey knew the password so it was private. Then he could watch snippets of the action whenever he had a break from the meetings. And watch the whole thing later tonight in his hotel room.

⸺●⸺

ZOEY AND GREG WERE on his bed, making out. They were still mostly dressed, except their shoes were off, and Greg had pulled her top up above her bra. He was cupping and squeezing her breast through the filmy lace of the bra. He reached behind and unsnapped her bra. He was getting better at it.

Zoey's hand was on Greg's hard-on. She was using her fingertips to trace the outline of his cock in his pants. She still couldn't believe his size. He was freaking huge.

Greg moved his hand down Zoey's body, over the flat of her tummy, and then onto her jeans. He moved lower, curling his fingers over her crotch. "Zoey ...," he said between kisses. "I think your jeans are wet."

She pulled away, surprise on her face. She reached down and touched herself. He was right, her jeans were moist. She was really wet. Was it possible her body knew how big Greg's cock was, and it was providing extra lubrication to accept it easier into her body?

They kissed. Greg cupped her bare, tiny tits, thumbing her nipples. Zoey reacted by arching her back and moaning, "Ah ah ah ...."

Then he ran his hand down her tight body, over her firm stomach, then back to her jeans. "Take them off me," Zoey said.

She raised her butt up to make it easier for Greg to peel the tight jeans down her long legs. When he saw the pantyhose he moaned.

"God Zoey, you're so sexy," he said as he ran his hands over her hose-covered legs.

Zoey though was impatient. She wanted him inside her!

"Pull them off me Greg," she said desperately. Greg did as she said. He pulled her panties off at the same time. He undressed quickly.

Now Zoey was completely naked. He was too.

Greg noticed she was still completely shaved there. "Shaving you was the hottest thing I've ever done in my life," he said as he kissed her.

He reached to her pussy, curling two fingers into her. Zoey groaned at this touch. "Zoey you're so wet," he said.

Zoey touched herself. He was right. She couldn't remember the last time she was so wet. She was so wet her thighs were moist. Her pussy throbbed, she wanted him inside her.

"Where are your condoms?" Zoey asked breathlessly.

Greg reached to his night table and pulled a condom from the box. He ripped it open and took out the circle of latex. He was about to put it on, but Zoey said "Here, let me."

She took the condom from Greg and then sat up and faced his manhood. She was curious about putting a condom on such a big dick. She pressed the center of the round condom against the head, and then tried to roll the latex down. Zoey struggled with it. It was hard to roll it down without ripping. Finally, she managed it. The stretched latex strained against his thickness, sheathing his tool like a second skin. And it barely made it halfway down his long shaft.

"Geez Greg, you are seriously big," Zoey said with awe as she stroked his cock up and down. It took both her hands to hold his manhood.

Greg moved to fondle her pussy again, but Zoey stopped him.

"No," she said. "I want you inside me know."

Through silent agreement, Zoey got on her hands and knees, and Greg moved behind her. Zoey reached back between her legs and guided his cock to her opening. Then as Greg positioned himself to thrust inside her, Zoey cradled her head in her arms, burying her face in his sheets. She waited for the penetration, preparing herself for his thickness.

Greg found her opening, then he pushed in. Zoey groaned at the penetration, clenching her eyes shut and closing her hands into fists.

"God Zoey you are so tight," Greg said as he slowly pushed in.

Zoey was incredibly wet so it was easier this time. It was getting easier each time. But still it was a struggle. Her opening and canal were stretched wide around his thickness. It was uncomfortable at first, but Zoey was getting to like the sensation of being stretched, of being so full. Also, because she was stretched so tightly around him, she could feel every nuance of his cock, like the rounded head and the veins going up and down his shaft. It was an amazing feeling, especially as he rubbed against those girl pleasure spots inside her.

Greg pushed in a few inches, then pulled out. He pushed in a little deeper, then out again. He went slow, each time going in a little deeper.

"Oh wow, wow, wow," Zoey moaned. He was barely inside her, and yet, her pussy was tingling, shooting sparks outward throughout her body. "Greg, god, your cock feels so good inside me."

Then suddenly she came. Her climax slammed her like a heavy wave crashing down. "Oh shit! Shit!" she whimpered as her hands clawed at the sheets.

"Did you just cum?" Greg asked. He was motionless now, just a few inches inside her.

"Yeah, yeah," Zoey gasped. "Give me a second."

Zoey's entire body was tingling, and her head was spinning.

She had never cum so fast! And just from his cock! Another vaginal orgasm from intercourse! And he was barely inside her! He had barely moved inside her!

After composing herself, she reached back to him. "Come on," she said. "I want all of it."

Greg pushed in gradually. Eventually he was all the way inside her.

"Fuck just give me a second," Zoey said. She needed to get used to his size. Also, she just wanted to experience it. The sensation of being so stretched, and so full.

Eventually Greg began moving in and out, going slow at first, then faster, but never pounding her hard. Now he was hitting her g-spot, his long cock sliding back and forth over it. And also, his thickness tugged at her clit, rubbing both pleasure spots at the same time.

"It feels so good ... don't stop Greg, please don't stop," Zoey begged.

This time her orgasm was like an ocean wave, slowly building up to a crest. It stayed at that crest for what seemed like forever, feeling so good, making Zoey whimper at the pleasure. Her eyes actually teared up, the prolonged sensations were so intense. Then finally the wave slammed down, and her climax exploded inside her. Zoey screamed as the orgasm ripped through her body.

Downstairs in the bookstore, sitting in his office, Jacob heard Zoey scream. He turned the volume of the jazz music higher.

Greg flipped Zoey onto her back. At this point, she was incoherent, her body coated with a sheen of sweat and tingling all over. She was aware enough, though, to register that Greg flipped her over while still staying inside her. She knew Hudson wasn't able to do that, and immediately she felt guilty for comparing her fiancée to Greg.

But Zoey didn't have much time to think about it, because then Greg was fucking her hard. He was pounding her, and Zoey held onto his arms for dear life. Then Greg put her legs on his shoulders and fucked her even harder.

Zoey had been fucked hard like this before. In fact, Hudson often fucked her harder and faster. But getting repeatedly slammed by a massive cock was something else. She had never been fucked like this. Never taken so completely.

Downstairs in his office, Jacob heard Greg's bed rocking and the clear sounds of sex.

Zoey wailed as it seemed like the pounding would never stop. And then it happened again. She came again. It was the different angle, with her legs on his shoulders. Zoey slammed her fists into the mattress as Greg made her freaking cum again on his freaking huge cock!

"Oh shit, oh shit, god, god, god!" she cried as intense orgasmic pleasure slammed her body.

Finally, Greg came, adding his cries of passion to Zoey's. His sperm flooded the reservoir of the condom.

Greg collapsed onto Zoey. The lovers panted into each other's face.

Eventually Greg began pulling out. He moved slow, so the condom wouldn't fall off. His cock was softening, but Zoey's pussy was still stretched tight around him. As he slowly slid out, little jolts of pleasure sparkled through Zoey's body, like little orgasms. That was another first for her. Feeling orgasmic pleasure from a man pulling out of her. *Pulling out of her!*

Zoey put her hands out as in surrender. All this was almost too much. It *was* too much.

"Okay, wow, okay, okay ..." she said as she breathed hard.

"Are you okay?" Greg said as he looked down at her.

Zoey couldn't help laughing. Was she okay? Yeah, she was okay. She'd just gotten the best fuck of her life.

The. Best. Fuck. Of. Her. Life.

She didn't even know sex could be that good.

"Yeah, I'm okay Greg," she said, looking up into his eyes, the laugh still in her voice. Then she kissed him.

As they made out, Zoey forgot about her iPhone recording and sending the video to the private internet site.

Hudson and Zoey's story continues in ~~ Be Careful What You Wish For - Book 2

Don't miss out!

Visit the website below and you can sign up to receive emails whenever Pete Andrews publishes a new book. There's no charge and no obligation.

https://books2read.com/r/B-A-KWSAB-ESAYC

BOOKS 2 READ

Connecting independent readers to independent writers.

Also by Pete Andrews

Be Careful What You Wish For
Be Careful What You Wish For Book 1

Faithful Wife's Fall From Grace
Faithful Wife's Fall From Grace Book 1
Faithful Wife's Fall From Grace Book 2
Faithful Wife's Fall From Grace Book 3
Faithful Wife's Fall From Grace Book 4
Faithful Wife's Fall From Grace Book 5
Faithful Wife's Fall From Grace Book 6
Faithful Wife's Fall From Grace Book 7
Faithful Wife's Fall From Grace Book 8

Flash Of Stocking Collection
Wife Watching Game And Other Stories: Flash of Stocking Collection 1
Wife Dates Another Man and Other Stories: Flash of Stocking Collection 2
Losing My Wife To Another Man - Three Interracial Cuckold Novellas: Flash of Stocking Collection 3

Girls Who Belong To Other Men
Girls Who Belong To Other Men Book 1
Girls Who Belong To Other Men Book 2

Opening Pandora's Box
Opening Pandora's Box 1 - Jessie Plays For Her Husband
Opening Pandora's Box 2 - Ollie Watches His Wife With Another Man
Opening Pandora's Box 3 - Jessie Grows Closer To Roman
Opening Pandora's Box 4 - Jessie Loses Herself In Roman
Opening Pandora's Box 5 - How Can You Do This To Me?

Tiny Dancer: A Modern Romance
Tiny Dancer: A Modern Romance Book 1
Tiny Dancer: A Modern Romance Book 2

Standalone
Playing At Work Is Dangerous: A Reluctant Wife Story

9 798224 578573